Dating down

Stefanie Lyons

flux ®
Woodbury, Minnesota

First Edition
First Printing, 2015

Book design by Bob Gaul
Cover design by Ellen Lawson
Cover image by iStockphoto.com/21659601/©-1001-
www.youworkforthem.com/E0658
Vespa illustration by Justin Lawson

Flux, an imprint of Llewellyn Worldwide Ltd.

Library of Congress Cataloging-in-Publication Data
Lyons, Stefanie.
  Dating down/Stefanie Lyons.—First edition.
    pages cm
  Summary: Seventeen-year-old aspiring artist Samantha Henderson, eager to learn about life and to get away from her father's political campaigns and her stepmother, refuses to give up on her new boyfriend, "X," even after he proves to be trouble, damaging her friendships and introducing her to drugs.
  ISBN 978-0-7387-4337-0
[1. Novels in verse. 2. Dating (Social customs)—Fiction. 3. Conduct of life—Fiction. 4. Artists—Fiction. 5. Friendship—Fiction. 6. Family life—Illinois—Chicago—Fiction. 7. Chicago (Ill.)—Fiction.] I. Title.
  PZ7.5.L96Dat 2015
  [Fic]—dc23

                                                            2014045397

Flux
Llewellyn Worldwide Ltd.
2143 Wooddale Drive
Woodbury, MN 55125-2989
www.fluxnow.com

Printed in the United States of America

For all the girls who've dated down
and picked themselves right back up.

I will call him X.

X

for the reasons I crossed him out of my life.

X

for the number of times I plunged into self-destruction.

X

because his name would only give him a place in your mind
that he does not deserve.

We Begin

I check out
X
with stolen stares
after school
over coffee
under piles of books.

Café Hex—
        dingy
        yellow
        red
        gray
X—
        cool
        calm
        smooth
clashes with the warm colors.

Hex seems like a circus.
A messy, disorganized carnival.
Jinxed as if it
might go under any second.
Fold the tents and pack up
        the bearded lady.
X—
        stacks dishes
        wipes tables
        long arms
        glide over coffee rings.

Concentrating,
>he pours coffee
>as I pore over homework.
>Chemistry and Algebra.
>*Does* a *equal* b?
>*Or is* a *only a fraction of* b *when divided by point seven?*

I'm just a junior, but
I can't wait for art school

… where less is more
>less structure
>less law
>fewer fatherly obligations.

Pushing paint along canvas,
>my goals   my gouache   my drive.

Not part of the political push for: Senator Henderson.
Art is when it's all about me: Samantha Henderson.

I sip coffee
stare
across the café.

X leans his lanky frame
>crisscrossed
>against the counter.

Steaming pots of coffee
halo his head.

What brings me here over and over?
        The colors?
        The chaos?
        The cute new employee?

This circle of thought   swirls
                    round and round
in my brain.

X steps outside.
Does he smoke?
Or is his shift over?

I wonder. Work faster.
Finish my assignments before the
out of business
sign goes up and
the sideshow skips town.

The ringmaster is leaving!
Show's over, folks!

My cue to go,
        he's no longer around to fill my cup.
My hope to return,
        he'll be here, same time and table.

As for what's next?
        My canvas awaits.

One Day at Café Hex

I ask if there are any chocolate muffins.

X

       plops down
       across from me
       smelling of lemons and tobacco.

       Delicious.

I feel studious and stupid.
My palms dampen.
I dry them on my jeans.

His nose sports a cast,
a post-party drunken fiasco.
Unsuccessful friends—mostly girls—signed
the tiny clump of plaster
       Mara
       Rose
       T.J.
       Jess
leaving a galactic pattern of purple ink
between his eyes.

His cheeks—warm? embarrassed?—blotch with red.

       My favorite color.

I stare
past his cast
into his eyes.
We chat.
His eyes shine
vulnerable-yet-experienced
>*An older boy stopping to talk to a high school girl.*

A mellow-type guy floating for a while—him.
A meticulous-type girl studying for finals—me.

X: I do what I please.
Me: I can't seem to please anyone.
Thinking of my father's motto—
>*If you can try, then you can try harder.*

His eyes
hover over me like a spaceship
searching for a safe place to land.
They
survey my books, my notes.

This isn't the real me!   I want to say.
I'm a painter! An artist!   I want to say.
Me: I have finals.

He shifts his weight
and the luster in his eyes fades.
>*Does he think I'm naïve since I still live out of a locker?*

One semester of college
and he had to take the next few off.
No money.
All twenty-two years of him, strapped for cash.

X: Life's really the learning experience.
Me: I want to learn about life. All of it.

He changes the subject to
                his friends' band   his apartment with them
                a party they threw   his hangover
                coffees at noon   writer, drummer, bass player
                the song they wrote   a poem he riffs

                He's a free spirit living a true artist's life.
So much more interesting than
Ted.
Athletic-headed Ted.
Immature,
emotionally dead
Ted.

So much more interesting,
X.
College-boy X.
Older,
indie, hipster
X.

I know nothing about his world
        living on his own
        bands
        underground parties
        no longer being a teenager
I only know mine.

And mine,
isn't that interesting anymore.

The Life

Livin' the life.
The less-than-stressful life.
The paint-my-own-fate life.
Canvas covered in
cafés
coffee
cream and sugar?
oil and acrylic?
Frida O'Keefe
Claude Gauguin
Pablo Warhol
My going-all-night
'til-nothing's-left
wrong-or-right life.

A life.
Alive.

Up in the rafters of freedom
down at the dive
bar none
havin' fun
footloose and fancy free
homework free
high school free
be all I can be in Bohemia

painting the town
painting my day
painting the night
My own post-modern impression
unrated, full-frame, opening night
at the gallery
       life.

Oh I wish I were ...
       ... livin' my life.

Consulting April, pt. 1

PickupPickupPickupPickupPickupPickupPickupPickup

April's phone goes into voicemail:
> *I'm out being fabulous. Leave a message.*

Since when is April a gal about town?
A gal about

       eyeliner—yes

       comfy jeans—sure

but fabulous?
The ever-shifting landscape of my friend.

I do as I'm told.
Me: It's me, Sam.

          Was just at Hex and wanted to—

My phone beeps.
April.

Before I can say hello, she's off and running.
April: How dare he …

          what a lump …

          taken for granted …

          honestly, Sam, he's too much!

The Problem with Ralph.
A topic usually reserved for

                                school hallways
                                        the cafeteria
                                                Chemistry
                                        English
                                Study Hall
                        locker rooms
                before final bell
        after pep rallies
and daily texts.

In other words ...
                I give my basic speech.

Me: He's a dolt ...
April: You're right!
Me: Doesn't care ...
April: I know!
Me: He's rotten.
April: He is!
Me: You can do better,
           speaking of better ...
April: I can!
           So, what's up?

I feel dizzy with excitement.
New-boy jitters.
I inhale just as April's phone beeps.
It's Ralph.
Me: I thought you just said—
           She puts me on hold.

           What good is a life on hold?

                        ...

Consulting Gavin, pt. 1

Gavin: Oh Henderson, why do you hang out in such
seedy places?

Me: Seedy? It's a coffee shop.

Gavin: Barney's has a coffee shop.

Me: And very expensive clothes.

Gavin: Exactly!

Me: That's not why I called.

Gavin: You met a guy!

Me: How'd you know?

Gavin: I'm all-knowing.
Is he cute?

Me: He's older. And tall. Very tall.

Gavin: And cute?

Me: Yes, he's cute.

Gavin: As cute as George?
Because, George is dreamy.
Isn't George the dreamiest?

Me: A real dreamboat.

Gavin: Great. Now we've got that settled.

Why are my friends so annoying when in love?

Gavin: So, he asked you out?

Me: What's with the twenty questions?

Gavin: I'm curious! ... I'm nosy!

Me: Thought you were all-knowing?

Gavin: I'm waiting ...

Me:	No, we just talked.
Gavin:	When he does, make sure he pays.
	You're worth it.
Me:	Don't be archaic.
Gavin:	College boys should pay.
Me:	He's not in college.
Gavin:	You said he's older. Do we need to talk about this?
Me:	No! He's college age. Just not in college.
Gavin:	Then what's he doing?
Me:	Working.
Gavin:	Good! So he can afford to take you out!
Me:	He's laid-back. And cool.

Gavin gasps.

Gavin:	He sounds adorable!
Me:	I think he is.
Gavin:	Then have him take you somewhere other than that grimy café.

Home

I take the long way home:
>   Division Street to Western Ave.
>   My stretch of Chicago.

I receive sisterly questions:
>   Where were you, Sam?
>   How come you didn't call?
>   Did you take Angie Hippo off my bed?
>   I'm telling Mom.

She's Jane.
And she's not my mom.

I trail behind the household police:
>   Melanie.
>   a.k.a. My five-year-old sister.

I walk through the family room:
>   *Vote Henderson!* signs

I see—
>   Jane.
>   a.k.a. Queen Vanilla.

pixie cut	properly combed
pearls poised	on collarbone
make-up made up	diamond studs

She's camera ready.
A posture-perfect picture of primness.

Dad: Samantha, where have you been?
Me: Thinking.
Dad: You're seventeen. How much you got
         to think about?

Funny guy.

Suggests I "think" about attending his upcoming rally.

Dad: Miguel wants the whole family there for pictures.

Primness and rallies—
         Equally fake.
         Falling fast out of fashion.

My father fawns over Queen Vanilla feigning a
         back ache   headache   something ache
for attention.

Jane: Dinner will be ready in ten minutes, Missy!

Name's not Missy …

I wrinkle my nose at Jane who's pretending to be
         head of the house
         sitting upright
         uptight
         in her chair
         trimming and folding
         trimming and folding

...
16

her campaign contribution.
I bound
up the stairs
thinking it'd be funny
if her perfect pearls
or other jewels
suddenly went missing.

… and you're not my mom.

My Mom

My mom is, graceful.
   Her long, wispy limbs balance dishes while dancing.
With standing ovation, I watch a wine glass rest on her head
    dazzling
      vibrant.

My mom is, doting.
   Her grand gasps and glowing accolades, hang on my
   artwork.
With reassurance, I gladly give up my Gauguin imitations
    encouraging
      visual.

My mom is, lively.
   Her kinky curls jump as she cracks kooky jokes.
With fascination, I join her clever chorus of "knock knock…"
    witty
      vivacious.

My mom is, dead.

Politician for the People

Before he was a
          politician for the people
my father was a
          devoted son-in-law for Grandpa's business
          coach for my soccer team
          study partner for spelling bees
          supporter for opening Mom's ballet school
          cheerleader for my report cards
          jokester for April Fool's Day
          pizza pusher for movie night
          storyteller for bedtime
          doting husband for his sick wife
          dedicated dad for his only daughter.

But now,
he can't be all those things
          for me
          and
          for everyone else.

For the People — Miguel

My father's favorite helper.
His little lackey.
My surrogate brother,
as Dad likes to say.
Miguel
> makes everything go away
> > or come to life

rushing and researching   recommending and reporting
rephrasing and reworking   rebutting and rebuilding
relabeling and realigning   reacting and readdressing
> recouping damages
> repairing reputations
> rewording stump speeches
> reviewing voter turnout
> restructuring schedules

rethinking and rethinking and rethinking and rethinking.

He's a fixer of problems.
He's along for my father's political ride.
And he's doing it all while receiving his M.B.A.
> restructuring his classes
> refusing a social life
> reassessing his career path
> repeating the mantra
> > *A politician for the people, not payoffs!*

He's focused and fearless
and sometimes I wonder,
> *Is it ever rewarding?*

For the People — Sam

Some of the people
        mainly this person
is for a particular future,
my future.

For the People of Me!

Preparing for senior year—
college at RISD
East Coast bound
Rhode Island and me
where I will learn to be
my own masterpiece.

Setting my goals
setting my sights
painting my way into my own
picture.

In My Bedroom

I set up a fresh canvas.
Study the stark surface.
Prepare for an email from Gavin:
> *When can I meet this Romeo?*

Or pseudo-apology from April:
> *R U mad at me? Don't be mad at me!*
> *I had to take Ralph's call, right?*

I place pink paint
onto the pale canvas
    feet dancing   plié   pirouette   lifting tip to toe
like Mom used to teach.
Not Jane.

A tiny hint of yellow, I
outline the edge of my shoe.
My ballerina shoe.

While the paint dries, I
open my laptop.
My BFFs both email.
I know them so well.

Gavin: *Let's face it. I must meet this dreamboat.*

April: *Sorry to ditch your call for that rat.*
            Ralph's a rat, right?

My Gavin

my go to
my guru
my glue
my *Green isn't your color*
my Geronimo
my GPS
my getaway
my gouache pusher
my Gwen Stefani
my Google
my Gatorade
my gossip column
my gaydar
my gems of wisdom
my granite
my gut instinct
my Geico insurance
my get-'er-done
my gofer
my guardian angel
my goalie
my German Shepherd
my girlfriend
my guy friend
but not

      my boyfriend.

April

She's flighty
funny
super bossy
fantastic busybody
flair for drama
and hair color
lip gloss
baggy shirts
and cool-girl kicks.

She loathes pretentious words like
ergo, nouveau riche, lexicon,
loquacious (although she is)
and describing people as fabulous
(apparently until now).

She's constantly changing
constantly obsessed with her
boyfriend
not-boyfriend
boyfriend
not-boyfriend
boyfriend
not-boyfriend
problems with Ralph.

She's the cheeriest person in every
hallway, classroom, café, lunchroom, gymnasium,
theater, shopping mall, taxi, or bus
unless, of course, she's discussing
The Problem with Ralph.

Regardless,
she's the world's most loyal friend.

The problem with Sam

Sam washes dishes.
She babysits her sister.
She folds her socks.

Sam saves her money.
She makes her bed.
She flosses.

Sam applies for college.
She wears clean underwear.
She washes her hands.

Sam studies for finals.
She eats her broccoli.
She waxes poetic.
She waxes the kitchen floor.
She attends political rallies.

Sam aims
Sam shoots
Sam misses

her
life,

love.

Next Time I See X

I'm in my favorite faded black jeans,
Gauguin's *Woman with a Mango* T-shirt,
pink and purple charm bracelet,
and my Chuck Taylors.
I'm indie and girlie
        at Café Hex.

Pretending to read
Life of Gauguin
I study the paintings
and X's flushed cheeks.
I'm stealthy and artsy
        at Café Hex.

He stops by my table.
X: After my shift, can I accompany you home?

He really says *accompany*.
No high school boy would *accompany* me.

Certainly not Ted.
Jock-head Ted.
High school Ted.

It feels chivalrous, so I agree.

Walking and Falling

We walk
down the tree-lined streets of Bucktown.
Sweet gardenias
blooming from balconies.
Sidewalk cafés
sprouting from nowhere.
Chicago in spring.

We talk
over the finer points of coffee.
Countries and climates
where beans come from
tasting bitter,
tasting bold.
X and me.

He wants to ride his Vespa
through the coffee fields of Columbia.
A tendril of hair flies in his face.

I tell him how I
        hate Geometry
        love Gauguin.

X: Sam Henderson. Smart *and* artistic.
Hearing him say it, I actually feel it.
        Artistic.

I can say   anything   everything   nothing
and he will understand.

      Are high school boys really that difficult to talk to?

Or
maybe I forget myself when he

                      looks at me.

Secrets

It only takes his look
                a glance.
And suddenly, shivers
                a need.
I need to share my secret dream
of painting in Paris.
Even though I know my dad would think it dumb.
            Flitting off to Paris to paint?

Me: I want to be an artist.
X: Looks like you already are.

He taps the Gauguin book in my arms
making me feel like a canvas
crisp and new
waiting for the acrylics.

It only takes my smile
                a grin.
And suddenly, candor
                a confession.
He swears he's never shared his dream
of a media empire like Hugh Hefner's.

His laugh is stealth,
like the funny things he says
just slip out the side, unnoticed.

X: Not the naked girls, of course. His media empire.
He smiles again in that way.
X: Hef changed the way people looked at stuff.
          I'd like to do that.
His sideways gleam
sets the butterflies free in my stomach.

Who is this boy with these charms? These
beguiling gazes, languid movements
and crazy-new thoughts?

A breeze sweeps through the trees.
We stroll down the sidewalk. Me,
not wanting to ever reach
home.

In Flux

We pass a faded blue car
resting like Rip Van Winkle.

Rust spots eat their way through the fender
the front wheel's locked down by the boot,
tickets wallpaper the windshield.

X's car.
An Oldsmobile Rocket.

Says he loves old stuff   records   vintage shirts
he touches my T-shirt
Is he flirting?
                      and cars.
He looks longingly at his.
I can't tell if his touch is light or loaded,
he's still looking at his car…
X: She doesn't run right now so I'm storing
           her on the street.

His cheeks flush
        pink
                crimson
                      burgundy.

His jet-black hair flops to one side.
He tucks it back like he's folding a blanket
hand to hair   tuck behind ear   repeat.

Two guys pass us.
Guys: Great party.
They pat X on the back   smile at me   walk on.
People know him   like him   party with him.

He places his hands in his pockets,
bows his head.
Is he embarrassed to be with me?

I study his
T-shirt   faded   hole starting along the sleeve
shoelace   untied   trailing as we walk.

His life is—
          in a cast
          in the boot, or
          in flux.

In flux.

Much more exciting than—
          in high school
          in political rallies
          in finals week.

Me: Well, this is me.
X: A brownstone.
He nods, flicks his hair.
Melanie peeks out from behind our bay window.

X: Your sister?

Melanie rests her face against the glass, staring at us.

Me: She came with the house.

X: You're funny.

            Inside my head,
I throw a party for my brilliant wit.
            Outside my head,
I smile.

X: So, want a lesson in coffee-tasting next time?

I nod, casually.

Neurons snapping in my brain.

            A date?
            A date!
            A date?

A date.

Saturday afternoon
            casual   cool   cups of coffee.

X: You're going to love it.

He winks

I smile

hoping I'm also not blushing

    pink

            crimson

                    burgundy.

Me: Okay. See you Saturday.

Half Full

cup cup
fill me up

hot steamy beverage caffeinating
        my heart

like an extra large latté you foam
        my brain

dreaming of nothing other than the

taste of your lips
        on mine
the smell of your hair
        brushing by
the heat of your shoulder
        bumping me

percolating under my skin

your dangerous smile keeping me up all night
        like a strung-out mess
filled to the brim and still thirsty
        for more.

I drink it all in
and wait for
you
to pour me
another

cup cup

At School

April looks at me, knowingly
shifting her pile of books
staring me up and down.
April: So, who's the boy?

She's good that way.

Gavin tips his bowler hat to us as April whines—
            I'm shutting her out
            storing secrets
            she knows there's a new love
            and he's not Ted.
            What gives?

Gavin: You didn't tell her about the old guy?
Me: Don't be jealous.
April: Old guy? Am I missing something?
Me: He's in college, well, was.
Gavin: And tall. And cute.
I blush.
Me: He is cute. And a free spirit.
April: Free spirit?

Ted walks by,
arms around some
sweet-looking sophomore
speaking softly, saying something sports-related
probably.

He   spots me
                    stops smiling.
I   pretend not to notice.
Ted can move on, right?

Feeling my nervous energy,
April springs into action—
                    Where'd you meet X?
                    How old is he?
                    How cute?

Then inevitably,
something triggers her into a story
about Ralph.
She is, after all, obsessed with Ralph.
Clueless, clueless Ralph.

April: He lives with musicians?
                    Think their band's as good as Ralph's?
Here we go.

I listen to *The Problem with Ralph*
up two flights of stairs and
through the final bell.

There will be more
to come on this subject
at lunch.

This is as certain
as homework.

High School Ted

High school boys play with toys they are, yes, they are that young. High school boys play with toys they are, yes, they are that young. I don't know why they like to play with toys, act like boys, make loud noise just to annoy us, when the girls are growing up. They play with toys it gives them joy, but girls don't see the fun. It's not fun, no longer fun. It's dumb. How come they enjoy it? High school girls like to shake their brain, bounce their curls. They want a guy not a boy. They want to flirt. What's the hurt? They want to court. Go out in short skirts. Paint the town red. Go head to head. But mostly what they want to do is anything and everything and something else but be with that boy, that high school boy, Ted.

Chemistry

Mr. Tanner scribbles
>*Antoine Lavoisier*

on the whiteboard.

April looks at me like,
>*Who the heck is that?*

She really should crack open a chemistry book.

Mr. Tanner scratches,
>*conservation of mass*

and faces the mass of blank stares.

Mr. Tanner scribes,
>*mass that's isolated cannot change over time …*
>*remains the same … unchanged.*

As Mr. Tanner explains,
I contemplate my own chemistry.
>*What is X doing right now?*
>*Is he sitting at some other girl's table?*
>*Is he thinking of me?*
>*Is he working right now?*
>*Or hanging out with his roommates?*
>*Is he doing twenty-two-year-old stuff?*
>*Artsy stuff?*

He's certainly not doing
Chemistry class stuff—
listening to a teacher
with male-pattern baldness
ramble on about matter.

And what matters is our chemistry.
But how could X possibly connect
with a high school girl?
A girl like me?
An isolated mass waiting to be unstuck.
                    Changed.

April passes me a note.
Carefully, I uncurl the paper and read it.
Another quandary over Ralph.

            Talk about bad chemistry.

Lunch

We are the usual suspects
at our typical table.
April slides in first
Gavin snuggles up to George,
squeezing some room for me.
I plop down my lunch of
> Twizzlers
>
> PB&J
>
> Chex Mix
Twizzling and crunching as
The Problem with Ralph, Pt. II begins.

April: What comes after this?
George: What's the big deal?
Gavin: What's a few drugs among friends?
April: I just don't see how we can be together when—
Gavin: You aren't together!
George: You aren't together!
Gavin and George make goofy love eyes at each other
for their same response.
Me: Can somebody clue me in here?
April: Ralph's doing—
Gavin: Things.
Me: Things?
Gavin: Bad things.
Me: Bad things?
I sound like a parrot.

April: Drugs, okay? Ralph's a druggie!

George: Honey, please! It's just pot!

April: For now, it's pot.

George: Plenty of people smoke pot.

Gavin: You do pot?

George: Sure! Now and then.

Gavin: Oh? And what else do you keep from me?

Gavin deflates.

Up next—*The Problem with George*, perhaps?

April: Hello! Can we focus on me?

I focus on April,

tell her it's not a shock

really

Ralph being one of the most

unmotivated guys I know.

Me: You're dating someone beneath you.

Gavin: Date up, honey, not down.

Me: You could do better, perhaps.

Gavin: Sam's right.
         Ralph's not so high on the dating scale.
         Get it?!

Gavin laughs at his play on the word "high."

George rolls his eyes.

April looks pained.

I finish my Twizzlers.

April: Well, when I get ahold of his supplier…

George: When you get hold of his supplier, give me a call.

He finishes his tuna casserole
                    winks at Gavin
                              walks out.

Gavin: People who do drugs are lame.
Me: People who deal 'em are lamer.
April: Is "lamer" a word?
The usual suspects all leave.

Then it's just me,
              my Chex Mix,
                        and my thoughts
                                  of April and Ralph.

Dating Down

Meet a guy
butterflies

then come lies
systemized

feeling low
can't let go

loss of spark
deep in dark

wonder how
this fell down

Once was great?
Break-up fate!

lesser highs
louder cries
greater price
major vice
loser guys
make life

      a
      sadder life.

Relationships, pt. 1—The Good

Gavin and George aren't afraid
to hold hands after class.

They share hats
and split chocolate bars.

They study together
and text all day long.

Gavin boasts about George's singing voice
George brags about Gavin's knack for math.

They smile a lot, flirt a ton,
and joke with each other constantly.

Gavin never seems out of sorts
when George is around.

Love.

Relationships, Pt. II — The Bad

April's mad about Ralph.

She follows him down the hall after class
bakes him brownies when it's his birthday
and sugar cookies when it's not.
She's sweet on him.

Ralph gives her a smile
gives her a hug
gives off no indication that he's as crazy about her
as she is about him.
Just enough interest
to reel her in.
>   *I like your hair like that.*
>   *You been working out?*

April's caught on his line.

She studies him instead of Chemistry
leaves him love notes
and donuts for breakfast.

Ralph runs off with his friends,
promises to call.
She waits for a ring when we're
                    at the mall
                    at a show
                    getting manicures
                    making dinner
                    listening to music
                    on the bus
                    out and about
                    settled in

Longing.

Relationships, Pt. III — The Lonely

My mom used to tell me stories
love stories
stories of her youth
her courtship
how she and Dad ran around
two peas in a pod
a daring duo
paramours
birds of a feather
lovebirds
fanning the flames
falling in love
forever and ever linked
together.

How she told it:
    eyes sparkling
            smiles emerging
                    memories bubbling
                            up from a place
                                    deep within her heart.

                            Will I find this?
                            Can I have this
                                    with X?

Back in My Bedroom after School

Me,
my canvas,
and thoughts of X's
> russet-brown eyes
> mahogany lips.

Will he call me before Saturday?
It's only Wednesday.
Does he miss me?
Do I miss him?
Did he ask for my number?

Maybe he'll
go online, look me up.
Maybe I'll
go online, look him up.

Round and round I go
red paint hits my canvas
lines begin bold,
> feather off.
It feels good,
> controlling color.
The playlist on my computer
s h u ff l e s
swift sounds
LOUD, **bright!** colorful sounds.
> *You, dear red,*
> *start and stop my head*

What's he doing?
What's he thinking?
Is he thinking of me?
Not thinking of me?

Do you know, sweet blue?

He's not thinking of me!
Is it true?

Oh, brown,
turn my thoughts around

He's thinking of me. It must be!
But, if it's not true—

I'm back to blue

Am I on his mind at all?
And if so,
    will he call?

Oh, pink,
I can't help but think

he will call.
But where will he be?
    what will he wear?
    what will he say?

Oh stop me, green,
from wondering

what he's doing
right now. Is he
walking
talking
eating
breathing
sleeping
or...

Round and round with
blue
brown
pink
green
red.

Colors, crisp in my head
my therapy

I, the painter
live the paint
b r e a t h e the artist's
life.

Dad

Lost in brushstrokes,
I jump when Dad lowers the "noise"
coming from my laptop.
He sits on the edge of my bed
    watching me   studying me   judging me
the usual.

Dad: Your art finals?
The *don't you want to be more than a painter?*
sound in his voice.
I nod and
continue painting.

Silence sits.

I could count on one hand the
number of times
he has said he's proud of me and still
have enough fingers left
to hold a cup of coffee.

I run a stiff stroke of cyan across the canvas.
It rests there like a lie waiting for truth.

Dad: Finished your homework?
I nod and
continue painting.

Dad: Don't you have a chemistry test this week?

Stroke stroke.
Stroke stroke.

Dad: Have you studied for that? Chemistry's essential
          for your SATs.

Stroke stroke.
Stroke stroke.

He leans back on the bed, gets
comfortable enough to take on a lecture.

Dad: Your mother and I ...
She's not my mother.
Dad: ... saving for your tuition ...
Dad: ... sacrifice ...
Dad: ... don't want to muck that up, do we?
Me: I studied, Dad.
Dad: That's my girl.

Pause.

Only time he's in my life
is to lecture me. Not like it used to be
with Mom.

The time before
>   cancer
>   funerals
>   elections
>   Queen Vanilla—
just us.

Blending the cyan with peach, I paint something pretty
something sweet
like the hands of a father
held out
holding his daughter.

Dad: Who was that boy who walked you home yesterday?
Me: Someone I met studying.
Dad: Seemed a little old for you, don't you think?
The politician's tone taints my portrait.

Stroke stroke.
Stroke stroke.

Never argue with a debater.

Stroke stroke.
Stroke stroke.

Me: Don't worry … head's screwed on … it's okay …
His contorted expression relaxes a bit.
A bit.
His phone beeps.

The usual check-in from Miguel.
Suddenly he's distracted,
engaged in Miguel's message.

Dad: Well, keep your nose to the grindstone.
        You're a Henderson and we Hendersons—

        Fingernails   across   chalkboard.

He rephrases.
Dad: Just remember, the primary's coming up.

Daddy's Girl Goes

Up in smoke
smashed small and
smothered smelling his pipe
his weathered hands his
worn watch and waiting eyes.

DADDY'S GIRL GOES

To the river
writhing wretched and
ready to catch a trout yank the line
pull out applause see his eyes
approving.

DADDY'S GIRL GOES

On his lap
taps his leg leaning
lanky and lurking up against
his chest keeping emotions close to
the vest.

DADDY'S GIRL GOES

Down to the ground
grown girl to glad woman where
whatever he says nothing
sounds safe so …

DADDY'S GIRL IS GONE.

The Girl

I paint flesh tones of a girl
asking something with her eyes
while her legs carry her away.
       I stare at the girl
       staring back at me.
What's on her mind?
What does she want?
What does she need?
       I don't know.
       I just paint.

I hear the cries of another girl
barreling into my room
while hugging her hippo.
       Melanie stares at me
       as she sways like a swing.
What's on her mind?
What does she want?
What does she need?

She wraps her slobbery fingers around my thigh,
points at my painting
nosy as ever.

Me: It's a girl.

I want to say *me*, but
I see her look
longing
lustful for the *me*
to be *her*.

Me: It's you.

Melanie smiles
sucks her fingers
buries her head in my leg
happy to be *her*.

>Is learning to lie, part of
>learning to love?

Sisters Seem

Sisters seem
        the same

grown in the same
garden
under the same roof
        watered and blooming
        out of the same ground.

Sisters share
        DNA

weeded out of the same
silt
tangled in the same family roots
        both reaching up to the sky
        to blossom in the sun

from different
sides
of the tilled
soil

iris and crocus
pollinated and cut
        from the same cloth
                        fragrant   fragile   flora
only
        not
        the same
        flower.

Coffee in Paradise

Indie coffee shops are like people,
no two are alike.

I meet X in a hot, new, halfway hidden
alcove.
Droopy trees
heavy with flora and leaves
hang over garden chairs.
Essence of java teases the air like forbidden fruit.

X, consumed in conversation,
pulls his hands out of his pockets
puts something in a stranger's hand
who hurries away.
My stomach flip-flops as I approach,
a testament to my excitement, I decide.

I say hello, wearing my
I'm trying really hard not to seem high school look.
Particularly tough to pull off after
filling out forms and finishing finals
then losing my way.

I couldn't find this café,
until right before my eyes it appeared
from nowhere
like an apple in Eden.

X wears his usual flushed cheeks,
tousled hair.
He shoves bills in his wallet as
I slide into the booth
plop my bag
tuck my hair
fold my hands like a prayer.

I'm right where I want to be
today.

Flavors

X orders a tasting menu of coffees.
We sip …

SWEET:

X: Most girls like sugar.
Me: Maybe I'm not so sweet.
         X smiles.

BITTER:

X: You're cute.
Not *hot* or *sexy*.
Cute.

         Are college girls sexy
         and high school girls just cute?

BOLD:

He points to a note pinned to my bag.
It says,

         Feed Alex and send me that link for the shoes.

Me: That's from my friend Gavin.
I sip slowly.
X: Does Gavin always pin nonsensical notes to your bag?
Me: He thinks it's ironic to be my mom.
I swallow.
Me: He's my best friend, actually. He likes shoes.
         And he's gay.

X: Who is Alex?
Me: My ivy. I forget to water him.
Carefully, I remove the *Vote Henderson!* sticker
slapped on the opposite side,
hide it in my pocket.

MILD:
He stretches arms across the wobbly table.
Fingers touching the back of my hand.
Grinning. Glancing.
That damn grin. Subtly, it melts me.

I take a sip of one—sweet, silky, smooth.
And another—earthy, citrus, bright.

So many flavors.
So many flavors I never knew…

Returning to Paris

Across from X
I envision the future,
sipping French Roast along the Seine.
           Could we?

Visiting Versailles on his Vespa.
I'd paint in a pretty loft,
prize-worthy paintings
sold outside the Louvre.

Fluent in French.
Living joie de vivre.

Artists
           photographers
                       bands
                                   and X.

It's a great feeling—
living
           sipping
floating
pretending
dreaming.

Dutch

We finish our fourth cup,
so jittery I can barely stand up
liquid insanity coursing through me
caffeine jitters
first-date nerves.

I tap my fingers on the table,
X's hand covers mine
replaces the tapping with an electric current
that shoots through my body.
One simple touch.

He suggests we go to Leo's for lunch
then reaches for his wallet.
The waiter flies to our table
quicker than a politician's promise.
I insist we go Dutch.
X: I can pay, you know.
He looks perturbed.

Does he think I think he can't pay?
Did I say the wrong thing?

I close my wallet
thinking of Gavin
and give up the Dutch.

Walking to Leo's

X's stride is long.
His lean limbs
lanky, look like weeping willows.
He plucks a geranium from a planter.
X: For you.

I close my eyes,
inhale.
A distinct, lemony-rose scent
rushes from my nose
to my heart
to my brain—
        Mom's perfume.

The one she used to put on
before she went out,
before—

I compose myself as he flicks his hair.
X: Like morning sun, it wafts. Desire. In the air.
        The smell of me. After touching you.
        I breathe in the ecstasy of love true.

A lyric. From one of the guys he lives with.

This is quite possibly
a moment out of a movie,
not one I'm living.

He offers
       a feeling
       a thought
       a random lyric
       a flower.
Can it always feel this good?

With Ted, love was
       help with homework
       Slurpees from 7-eleven
       a lukewarm letter jacket.

I sniff the geranium as we pass a tire shop.
Guys covered in grease watch.
When the traffic light turns red, we cross.

They are
waiting in cars
wanting to move on.

I am
walking on air
wanting time to stand still.

Leo's Lunchroom

One gentle scoot
        into the booth
side by side
        smile   blush   bump
two hips collide.
Like atom bombs
        flatten countries,
my skin collides
        with his kinetic energy
and lands
in a mushy clump of
        happily   ever   after.

Take that, Antoine Lavoisier!

Another waiter
        and an order later,
fed and full
        soda   soup   sandwich
X holds his napkin
folds a beautiful bird
        hands it to me.

X: Your first gift.
Me: First?
Will there be others?

One gentle scoot
        into the root
of my
        head   hands   heart.

What I Learn in Walking

After lunch,
X shows me a storefront window
stained with graffiti.
His dad's barbershop years ago—

>   broken barber chairs
>   torn seats
>   missing headrests
>   tipped over
>   brown squares on the wall where
>   mirrors hung

now gone
destroyed
ruined.

Me: What happened?

X: Cancer.

The Cancers

I thought I was the only one.

I tell him about Mom—*I was in grade school.*
And Jane—*My dad quickly remarried.*

He tells me about his dad—*Died when I was in junior high.*
And his mom—*Financing my father's treatments drained us.*

My mom. His dad.
We do the math—
       Our parents died within months of
each other.

We were strangers,
suffering
silently
at opposite ends of the city.

What I Learn in Sitting

A temporary ride with
permanent smiles.
Our bus trip to my house.

From this moment on, I will discover
    art
            life
                        people
                                  experiences
                                              myself
whether or not my suffocating father approves.

X: Life's a mystery.
Me: Yes. A mystery.

And then I see how
    studying
            obeying
                        pushing myself
                                  trying to be
everything Dad wants from me is just silly.

The bus spits me out on my street.
It's the perfect afternoon
with secrets sealing my heart to his.
Kismet, our connection.

Before I've even made it up the stairs, a text.
Cutie.

I gush.
Luckily, he can't see my face
     as red
               pink
                         crimson
                                   burgundy

as the canvas in my room.

girls' night

April wears all black
        fingernails
        lipstick
        eyeliner
        and hair
        newly dyed
        from its constant state of mousy brown.
The gods of Goth have taken her.

April: Just wanted to mix things up.
She's lying.
I smell a *Ralph*.

Me: You look good.
I'm lying.
I wait for the *Ralph*.

But I can't hold it in any longer,
blurting out—

      I think I'm in love!

Change of Plans

Just like that
in the midst of crossing the street
and retrieving her bus card,
April stops
swings around
switches direction.

Change of plans!

With one whip of her arm,
Whoosh!
we're in a cab
heading toward my future.

Lady Elba, Pt. 1

A red neon *open* sign shines
in a black window.
Dark, shady, Goth-esque.

A fortune teller leads us inside.
I feel crazy.
This is crazy.
She looks crazy.
Why are we here?
Has April gone crazy?

Pink tinted lenses
hair piled atop her head
like an uneven stack of plates.
This could topple any second.
        Lady Elba.

Her bony hand grabs mine I
      follow   stumble   trip
my way into my future.

Lady Elba: Let's see what's going on …
She lays a hand over my heart.
Lady Elba: … in here.

What's going on *in here* is a mixed bag of tricks.
Will she pull out the right trick?

She sits,
doesn't speak.
Lady Elba?

I shake,
don't believe.
Does April?

Placing my *aura* in her *presence*,
   opens my palms
        clasps my hands
                so different from X's grasp.

In spite of myself, I'm curious.
Lady Elba
lays out the cards
she tsks and hmms
      tsk tsk tsk
      hmm
like a sprinkler
or a typewriter—then gasps.

April: What?
We lean in.
A clock chimes.

Lady Elba: Something big…
She stares me down,
unnerving me with her crazy-lady look.

Lady Elba: Something big is ...
                    Is ... ?
                    Is ... ?
Lady Elba: ... on its way to your soul.

Her eyes sparkle.
Words whisper.
Lady Elba: Brace yourself, my dear.
The creeped-out side of me wrestles with the hopeful one.

April: How romantic!

I doubt.
Although, I wonder ...

How Big Is Big?

Like summer fling big?
Soul mate big?
Getting-married-moving-to-Paris-growing-old-together big?
Big enough to wrap its arms around me?
Bigger than a kiss?

How big is big?
Can it quiet Queen Vanilla?
Reverse the dying process?
Heighten the hues of paint on a canvas?

How big is big?
Can it eliminate anger? Bond father to daughter?
Cure cancer?
Is big more powerful than a political promise?
Greater than gossip with Gavin?
Huger than Angie Hippo?
Can it wipe out a conservation of mass with a wave of its wand?

How big is big?
And when it hits my heart,
will it explode?

How big
is

big?

Sunday Morning when
I Come Home from April's

Dad's
suited up
pacing in the living room
planning his position
practicing his speech.

Miguel's
following along
revising, rewording,
researching who said what when
and how to rephrase it.

Melanie's
in PJs and mismatched socks
scratching the peanut butter
in her hair.

Jane's
uptight
rushing into the den
grabbing papers, rubbing her neck
cursing as she throws
couch cushions on the floor.
Jane: Where'd I put that damn necklace?

...
81

I
take Jane's usual superior tone.
Me: Mothers shouldn't use such language.

My disapproval of Jane fills me with memories of Mom.
        At least mine didn't.
I
whisper while
covering Melanie's ears
en route to the bathroom
to clean her hair.

Melanie: What's a primercy?
Me: Primary.
I tell her it's a silly day where adults
wave things in the air
dress in costumes and pretend
they're so important.
        Vote Henderson!

Me: It's like Disneyworld for grown-ups.
        Only, there's no Mickey.

Jane peeks her head in.
Her perfectly lined lips
smudged ever so slightly.
Me: I'm cleaning Melanie's filthy hair.

My inflection suggests Jane should be ashamed.
She doesn't seem to notice
her mothering skills
taking a backseat to my father's big day
as they
try to persuade more chumps to
>*Vote Henderson!*
while their daughter marches
around the house—
>mismatched socks,
>messy face,
>matted hair.

I don't mind watching Melanie.
It beats going out on the campaign trail.
Me and Melanie, we
might just be
two peas
in the same political pod.

Miguel reminds Dad that it's time,
he's prompt like that.
Dad kisses our foreheads.
Dad: Wish me luck.
Melanie: Luck!

Melanie stares at me after they leave.
>*Does she know her mom's alive*
>*and mine's not?*

Fade to Nothing — Jane

She
fades like the shade of gray
into the night
only, it's day.
What can you possibly give me?

She
wades like the waters of Lake Michigan
into my room
uninvited.
Why are you here?

She
preys like the panthers of the Serengeti
over my dad in
Mom's absence.
Who do you think you are?

She
plays like the perfect mother of Melanie
not me
in Mom's house.
When will you leave?

She
remains nothing
to me.

With Melanie

Push me!
           We swing.
Lift me!
           We teeter-totter.
Hold me!
           We slide.

I support Melanie on the monkey bars.
Only yesterday, I was Melanie and Mom was me:

     swinging   sliding   supporting

I love my sister, still, she's
a constant reminder that Dad has moved on:

     another marriage   another child   another woman
Making Mom a memory of   another time.

I tell Melanie about Mom.
How my mom   *looked.*
How my mom   *moved.*
Her graceful   *sway.*
Her dancer's   *stance.*
How we played   *hopscotch.*
How we burnt   *kettle corn.*

How we collected   *seashells*.
Painting each one a color of the rainbow.
Our lucky stash.

Melanie
thinks the stories are funny, inspiring.

Melanie
decides we should collect rocks
and paint each one a color of the rainbow.
Just like Mom and I used to do.

Melanie: Me and you.
Me: Just us two.

Rocks

Across the park,
we scour the grass for rocks—
       flat ones
       white ones
       round ones
       smooth ones
       big ones
       tiny ones
       lopsided ones
ones that past the test,
we put in our pockets.

In the park,
a guy's propped up—
       smoking
       drinking
       grimy
       yellow
       eyes aglow
       strung-out
one 40 oz. bottle,
he puts in his pocket.

Guy: Hey!
Must get Melanie.
Guy: Hey! You, girl.
Must get out of here.
Guy: Sam!
He knows my name?

I freeze, feeling like I might throw up breakfast.
I study his glassy eyes, skinny body:
> *The guy talking to X when we met for coffee.*
> *The guy who took off the minute I arrived.*

Why is he ...
        out here
                strung out
                        friends with X?

I do not know
but I grab Melanie
and we go.

Missy

A kitten follows us home
meowing like Little Orphan Annie.
>*Meow.*

Born on the streets
incapable mother
tossed from one alley to the next.
>*Meow. Meow.*

Life of despair and hardship
all alone.
>*Meow.*

Who can refuse such a sad story?
We watch it
cry and pace
sit in the middle of the sidewalk
watching us
watching it.

Melanie: Think it's a girl?
I shrug.
Melanie: I want her to be a girl.

We decide it's a girl.
Melanie names her Missy.

Melanie: So Mommy has a Missy.
Her rationale makes me smile.
I place milk on the back porch.
Melanie: Nighty-night, Missy.
She says,
holding Angie Hippo.

Phases

Missy moves in
Dad's campaign moves forward
X moves around Hex
    waiting tables   taking orders   pouring coffee.

I never ask about the guy in the park
Maybe I overacted
I watch X's
    long arms   flouncy hair   winks.

He knows all kinds of people
coming and going at Hex
interesting in their own way
    scruffy students   aging hipsters   young
                                                              businessmen.

Visiting X invigorates me
his friends make me feel less ordinary
inspiring
    new thoughts   new ideas   new paintings.

No longer drawing pale girls and soft hues
I choose
    darker images   edgier colors   bolder strokes.

I'm like April and her Goth phase
only, I don't want to come out of this phase
    today   tomorrow   ever.

Rockets

I bring X
banana candies from a corner store
mini handmade paintings
giant grins.

He hands me
a lyric he heard from his roommate
drawing he found
poem copied from one of the French masters.

Most times,
I wait for his shift to end.
He walks me home.

When we walk, we fall
into a rhythm
like the first time we passed his car.

Today,
he points to the Oldsmobile's rocket emblem.
I remember his initial flirty touch.
When I blush—
    pink
              burgundy
                    crimson

He puts his palms against my cheeks to
    cool them
    feel them
and my heart takes off
like a rocket to Mars.

First Kiss

On the sidewalk, my arms go limp. My neck tingles from his touch. The little hairs stand at the nape of my neck. The leaves rattle in the trees. My heart rattles in my chest. Fingers weave through hair. Thoughts run through head. Tingles surge through body.

He wraps me
close
closer
closest to him yet.
Something big is on its way...

He leans down
close
closer
closest to my face.
Something big is on its way to my soul.

His lips move, forming words. I'm unsure what they say. I cannot hear with the ringing in my ears. And the pounding in my chest. And the quickening of my breath. Wondering how this will happen. What it will feel like. Where do we go from here? That's when they meet.

His lips are velvety, plump,

mahogany   cherry   scarlet   vermillion   maroon   cardinal

red
> like a stroke across my painting

red
> like a fireball in the heart of a warzone

red
> like fingernails fresh from polish

red
> like the molten hot center of the Earth.

Soft   gentle   warm   long   rapturous   dizzying.

I breathe in through my heart and out my eyes. Until I can't breathe, kiss, feel, think, stand, see. Taking my hand. Walking me home. Reaching my front door. Holding his hands against my cheeks. Rubbing nose-on-nose with mine. We Eskimo kiss goodbye.

Something big has landed in my soul.

X: Call me after you finish your homework.
I nod, knowing full well
I'm spending the evening
not thinking of homework
only

his lips
        the sugary softness
his eyes
        the chocolaty warmth
his hair
        the citrusy scent.

No, not doing homework,
but I pretend to comply.

My happy lie.

Spaceship Cake

his smile, slanted,
a lopsided spacecraft
tilting time to one side
leaving me askew as
charm oozes out the cracks.

his eyes, dark,
orbital sugar-coated cones
spinning their mad power
slicing into me as
light, fluffy love seeps out the circles.

it's a double whammy
a one-two punch
an ambrosial spell

—a reverse—

like the earth orbiting the moon
stirred together and
baked
in a space-time continuum
unspoiled
weightless

call Nestlé!
alert NASA!
his buttercream lips hover
over my heart

and stars
and Mars
and moons
and galaxies
could melt into his kiss
just like
I have.

When I Visit His Apartment, pt. 1

I walk in
behind him.

The room sings
of zines and books
broken piano keys
alibis and secrets
bottles rest on Bukowski
like a side table
made of *Pulp*.

Wine corks nestle beside laptops
Velvet Underground propped against a ten-speed
a fern stares out the window.
Guitars—electric and acoustic
hang out.
There's a banjo.
A banjo?

X steps over a box, picks up a ukulele
strums it.

X: Sam, oh, Sam. Sweet, sweet Sam

Like a tune from a
Grammy-winning ditty, it's music
to my ears.

At last, I've found
a song
a boy
a place
I can sing along to
cuddle up beside
rest.

After we move the Wii and coffeepot,
sit side by side
on the couch
missing a cushion
we glide together, giddy, gulping up
laissez-faire.

Me: So this is what it's like inside.
X: Yep.

Our eyes sparkle into each other
hovering above
the dirty dishes piled up in the kitchen
across the room
the one
big room.

X: This is it.
He grins
and I can hardly believe he means the apartment.

The Meet — April

April comes with me to the café,
orders a vanilla latté
> sugar-free
> with soymilk
> and extra foam
> in a to-go cup

even though she's sticking around.
Could she be more high maintenance?

She giggles a lot
like she's the one with the crush.
The old giddy April,
bubbling out from underneath
> faded black hair
> brooding eye make-up
> dark fingernails
> crimson-stained lips.

X casts a simple spell
over April, he bewitches,
enchants.

The meet at Café Hex.

Her take—

> Seems so mature.
> Not like Ralph.
> Did you see all the people that came in just
> to talk to him?
> He's the café's biggest attraction!

I smile, happy to have won her approval.

The Meet — Gavin

It's Gavin's seventeenth birthday party.
Bring a date!
At the Sock 'n' Bowl
a Laundromat in the back
bowling alley in the front
'80s formals theme.

I show up with X.
Him—makeshift tux and Chuck Taylors.
Me—yellow corsage X got at his *special* flower shop.
It clashes with my purple and black dress
but complements my diamond earrings
the gems I took
from Jane's jewelry box
never to return.
My gift to me.

We sing *Happy Birthday*
then flasks come out
spiking sodas and juices
as moods lighten.
Time rolls by
as bowling scores decline.

Gavin: I get it.
Me: What?
Gavin: He's got that dangerous side.
Points to my wrist corsage.
Gavin: He five-fingered your flowers.

I tell him to stop creating stories.
Just admit it. You like him!

Gavin admits
          the flowers smell beautiful
          he has a flair for drama
          X isn't so bad after all.

Gavin: Although he mentioned using
          sleight of hand to acquire your corsage.
He buries his nose in my wrist bouquet.
Gavin: I could've misheard.
          He was on the phone.
Me: I'm sure you did.

And it's all good.

Just like I knew it would be.

Looking for Ralph

April: I can't find Ralph.

Me: Did you check the men's room?

April: I can't go in there!

We would ask Gavin, but he's busy
making out with George by the shoe return.

Me: What about the Laundromat?

X: I'll go look.

X disappears
as Ralph returns stinking of pot.
But before April can read him the riot act
X returns saying
he has to go.

Please tell me this boy is not dumping me in front of
all my friends. Leaving me
stranded and humiliated in front of my toughest critics.

Another party.
He'd committed to weeks ago.
Has to be there.
Imperative.
He feels bad.
Blah. Blah. Blah.

Gavin: Why don't we all go?

X wears this
        weird look   pained glance   nervous smile
then
we all go
to the party.

What a High School Party Isn't

Two-bedroom apartment
Wicker Park
three girls
zero parents
X walks through the door like he's home
me
Gavin
April
George
Ralph
follow him up the narrow staircase.
Noise grows
louder
louderlouder
louderlouderlouder
until we're greeted by
  cigarettes
  beer
  sweat
  sticky
  dense
  air
  wall-to-wall people
crouched on furniture
balancing drinks and cigarettes.
A wet film coats the floor.
My shoes leave prints in it.

Red plastic cups rest
in windowsills,
on tables,
tumbled over.

X sees a girl, leaves me there, stupid,
standing beside my high school friends
in '80s formals.

I try to talk to Gavin,
but the music's too loud.

I've been to high school parties before,
and high school this isn't.

Diamonds in the Rough

I'm a statue,
sweet
   solid
       stuck
              in a cheesy prom dress.
Could this get anymore uncomfortable?

People avoid us
either because we're obviously underage
or because it's too crowded.

As I place my corsage in my purse
a girl appears, admires my earrings.
Queen Vanilla's pillow-cut diamond studs.
I tell my new friend, Betty, they're fake.

Betty: You guys come from Prom or something?
Gavin: Tonight is cause for celebration!
Betty: Oh yeah?
Betty takes a long draw from her cigarette.
Gavin tells her it's his birthday.
Betty's friend, Madison, tells Gavin he's cute.
Betty: Madison loves the boys.
           So does Jessica.
She points to a girl flirting with X.
Betty: Good ole Hefner.

Eye roll   laughter   my head starts to ache.

Gavin: And you?
Betty: I'm not so easily won over.
Gavin takes Betty's comment as a challenge,
dances away with the ladies.

Me: He's gay!
I yell.
No luck.
They're drunk.
I'm stuck.
Besides, Gavin's great with girls
and, it appears
so is X.

Upon Where I Start Livin' the Life

George is MIA
Ralph is glassy-eyed
April looks anxious to go home
I do too, after seeing *Jessica*.

Don't want to drink
don't want to think
don't want a hangover
just want to paint.

Then X returns holding two red cups.
X: For my favorite new friend.
He gives one to April.
X: And my favorite female ever.
He leans in
   smells my skin
         tells me I'm a sexier picture
than anything some French Post-Impressionist could paint.

My heart pounds
   palms sweat
         thoughts race,
            so I drink up.

Burns going down
lightens me up
I relax.
X wraps his arms around me and we
move in and out of the crowd.

Quickly, I'm feeling fantastic
like Gauguin greatness
a million-dollar mural.
X chats with guys, girls,
high-fives something into their hands.

Everyone knows him
happy to see him
and because I'm with him,
happy to see me too.

I'm not a high school girl
crashing this party.
I'm the girlfriend of X and
I'm livin' the life.

The Bathroom

Drinking, drinking, I'm so thirsty!
Now I have to pee.

Waiting for the single bathroom,
I lean against the wall to see.

Blurry, dizzy, I'm so silly
knocking photos down.

> A crash.
> We laugh.
> *Ha ha ha ha ha ha ha!*

I fumble with the frame to hang it,
but oh so many nails.

Which one is the real one?
Which ones are the spinning ones?

I take the photo to the bathroom,
sit upon the pot.

An image of a little girl
holding her daddy's arm.

This must be a girl that lived here
before she threw these fetes.

She was just a little girl
who held her daddy's hand.

I close my eyes and think about this
until I get the spins.

Next, I vomit in the toilet
        Oops!
the alcohol wins.

I set the frame upon the sink
and leave to find my friends.

Bye-bye little girl so sweet.
Bye-bye daddy holding her hand.

With Gavin

4:30 in the morning
sneaking into Gavin's house
we shush each other quietly.

Gavin shushes me
   I shush April
         April shushes the door handle.

We tiptoe through the living room
down the stairs
to the basement,
Gavin's bedroom.
By shushing we become noisy.
Luckily, Gavin's parents are heavy sleepers.

Me: Happy Birthday.
Lying in the room
in a borrowed
T-shirt and sleeping bag,
I whisper to Gavin.
April's already asleep
snoring,
her black eyeliner smudged around her eyes.

I roll over, about to go to sleep when
my friend whispers
almost inaudible
very faintly
super quietly,
Gavin: I like him.

Does he want me to hear?
or not?

I close my eyes and dream of red plastic cups
stacked to the sky
forming
something big.

Freewheeling

On the last day of classes X pulls
into the high school parking lot
on a Vespa.

Everyone checks us out.
Even Ted mutters something
to one of his jock-head friends
        over his shoulder
        under his breath
        behind my back
        as I walk by.
I pretend not to hear him.
It's been over between us for ages.
Well, in high school time, that is.

Me: Nice wheels.
When did he buy a Vespa?
X: Just borrowing it.

And, off we go,
racing through the streets of Chicago
wind flying through the pieces of hair
wiggling out from under my helmet.
I think fast
fun
crazy
lawless
thoughts
as X speeds in and out of lanes
gliding
onto Lake Shore Drive.

X: You ready for this?
I wrap my arms tighter around his waist, kiss his neck.

This means *Yes*.

Yes

Wherever we're about to go
whatever we're about to do,
Yes.

Up Ashland Avenue
down West Webster
over a bridge,
Yes.

X signals with his arm because his blinker is broken.
In flux.

He takes off his helmet
pulls a latch
opens a square lid perfectly hidden within the bridge.

He jumps down
holds out his hand and
I follow him into the alcove.

Closing the lid—there we are—under the bridge
floating above the Chicago river.
Hidden away in our private Paris along the Seine,
Oui.

I gasp.
Before I can ask, X covers my lips with his fingers,
kisses me hard   wet   intense
causing a dizzy   warm   swirl
in my head.
Something big is on its way …

His hands run underneath my shirt,
unclasp my bra.
My hands move through his hair
and I pull
close
closer
closest
to him yet.

Sex

My bra
my shirt
the late-May air.

His hands
my body
the canvas of me.

The shivers
the glances
does he like what he sees?

He smiles a leaky smile
and I wonder—

> Am I like the wafting desire in his roommate's lyric?
> Am I still his *cutie*?
> Am I ready for what's to come?

Just then—a banging—people
walking over the bridge
over our heads
totally unaware that we're
under here
nestled in our own little built-in cubbyhole.
X: It's a secret maintenance area.
He touches me.
X: The city never locks the latch, so we have to be quiet.

It's public   private   totally sexy
        and that's when I know
all these things I probably shouldn't be doing
        I am going to do
because he is the one
who knows about these things
        painting the town
        footloose and fancy free
        livin' the life.

He pulls out a condom
    kissing me
          rubbing against me
              unzipping my pants
          and what we do next
    is one of the many things
I've been waiting to learn.
I follow his lead and
together we
crash
back and forth
bodies bumping slowly.
His kisses consume me, making me hot
warmed from the inside out.

A flame
    sparking
         igniting
              growing
        blazing
   thundering
shattering
all that's within me.
I feel closer to him than any other human.
His breath,
hot like lava
along my cheek.
X: God, I love you.
And then I melt just as he
shivers into me.

When we put our clothes back on and pop out of
our cubbyhole
the Vespa's being towed.

X watches it go.

That's when I learn
        the vehicle
            wasn't borrowed.
It was registered as
stolen.

Undone

light
f.light
flit
flo.at

I open my wounds
        and fin.d

they're healing

sealing my love
        to h.is
feeling his body
        on mine
reveal.ing the us
        in.side
the more I un.do
        my life
t.he more it reveals
        to me

undo
un.done
under
hi.m

Arrivals . . .

Summer begins like this—
> floating under bridges
> kissing in coffee shops
> napping in X's arms
> eating grilled cheese at Leo's Lunchroom
> attending packed parties in abandoned lofts
> arriving in the latest set of wheels

Where does he get them?
> meeting his friends, acquaintances, and strangers.

Everyone knows X
loves X
high-fives and peace signs X.
He's a celebrity in his circle
and I'm his girl.

I've arrived.

Although I'm way behind
on my painting deadline for RISD,
I'm way ahead on my life.

Missy
graduates from being a stray
that Jane and Dad will "think about keeping,"
to our cat, living in the house full time.

Melanie
mommies her, dresses Missy like a doll,
teaches her how to shake hands.

Me: The cat's not a dog.
Melanie: Shake, Missy.
Missy puts her paw in my hand.
We shake.

And that's how summer arrives.

... and Departures

Finals come and go
school lets out
no more passing Ted in the hall
pretending not to know each other
won't have to see him with
some dumb sophomore.
Good riddance.

George departs for L.A.
to spend the summer with his father.
His newly divorced parents live on
separate sides of the country
leaving Gavin also separated
and on the sad side.

Gavin: How will I live without him?
Me: It's just a few months.
Gavin: Might as well be forever.
Me: True. I wouldn't want to leave sunny Los Angeles.
Gavin: YOU'RE NOT MAKING ME HAPPY!
Me: Sorry.

Gavin's take is something straight out of *Casablanca*:

George   walks toward plane.
Gavin   in summer's new J. Crew seersucker jacket,
         begs George.
             But what about me? What about us?
             Tries not to cry.
             Opens man-purse, grabs tissue.
             Tries not to cry.
George   asks Gavin to be reasonable.
             We'll always have senior year.
             Kisses him goodbye.
Gavin   pleads with George not to abandon him.
             You get on that plane, leave me, and we're through!
             Tries not to cry.
             Cries.

My take is a little more straightforward:

Gavin gets upset at being alone all summer.
George tells him not to be needy.
Gavin's a needy guy.
         A tad dramatic.
George says as much,
Gavin cries.

Gavin swears that
         he's inconsolable
         George has ruined his life
         he'll spend his summer throwing darts at a map
         Cali will be the bull's-eye.

I feel bad for my Gavin
my pal
my heartbroken bud.
Here's looking at you, kid.

Just when one season begins
another one ends.

The Rally

Lounging at Hex,
I almost forget my father's big rally
until Miguel calls to remind me.
          Don't be late.
I run home
just in time to hear
Queen Vanilla on the phone.
          Can't take it anymore…
          It's just not right…
Probably talking to Dad.
Probably talking about me.

I ignore her as I race up to my room.
Melanie follows, cheering
as I throw off my clothes
dive into a dress
tear a comb through my hair
pile my locks
on top of my head.

I'm ready in   five
                    four
          three
     two
one

And, Action!

In a flash
I'm in a hotel ballroom
watching my father shake hands.
Smiles frozen on our faces
posed like a picture.

> *VOTE HENDERSON!*

Signs bob up and down in the crowd
Miguel hands Dad his speech
the energy in the room elevates
my heart quickens.

> *My dad is really loved.*

It makes me look at him differently, as
> a man
> a father
> a hard-worker
maybe he loves me in his own way.

He moves in and out of the crowd
> nodding
> smiling
> shaking hands.

> *That's my Dad!*

As he approaches me, I smile,

> spontaneous
> candid
> genuine

Dad: Your dress is a wrinkled mess.

I look down at my dress.

Dad: Why didn't you let Jane pick something out?

Miguel: A politician for the people, not payoffs!

Miguel works up the crowd
helps his own career.

Dad turns around and waves
breaking my family bliss
my happiness.

I stand stunned while Chicagoans chant this cheer.
What he stands for.

> *For the people, not payoffs!*
> *For the people, not payoffs!*

Then there's me, the people

> the wrinkled
> disheveled
> daughter.

> *We Hendersons have a reputation to uphold!*
> *Down with wrinkles!*

I can be the
          person
          daughter
          citizen
          Henderson
he thinks I'm supposed to be.
Even in a messy dress!
Only I know full well
I'm not.
I'm nothing like what he wants me to be.

          His daughter.
          His let down.

Choosing
painting over politics
partying over parents.

And if he had a clue about
what I do with X,
he certainly wouldn't approve of that
          person
          daughter
          citizen
          Henderson.

Henderson Family Wrinkles

How can I be
wrinkle-free
when I'm pressed with—
You should know better, try harder.

Inside my skin, my label reads—
40% honorable daughter
30% delicate girlfriend
15% resilient friend
10% supportive sister
and 5% I cannot iron out

       mom

I'm washed by the political machine
hung out to dry
colors running, bleeding into
the warm, salty, tear-stained water
leftover from the gentle cycle
worn out from our family fabric

I cannot sort it all—the dirty laundry
I cannot fold it up—my father's need
steam-cleaned genes
bunching at the seams
eating into my dress,
politically pressed
gathered at the hem of a
disappointed father
distant step-mother
clingy sister
    cycling   spinning   washing over me
like a love-starved stain
my dry-clean-only life

    blazers   pants
underwear and shirts

    folded   flat
delicate and pressed

    father   Jane
Melanie and me.

Chemo and Balloons

Dad speaks to the crowd
we sit
in silent support.

His nuclear family:
      Melanie
      motionless
      in ruffles and curls
      sucking her thumb.

      Jane
      properly pressed dress
      pearls perfectly placed
      around her neck.

Reminds me of her diamond earrings I gave away
to Party Betty.
One of the little ways I secretly take from Jane
and give back to Mom.

Dad goes
on
and on
about the wonderful things
he will do if elected Illinois State Senator.

      Why does he give so much to others?
      What about me?

It seems he's
less
and less
the father I knew with Mom,
more
and more
someone else entirely.

Am I someone else entirely, too?

I'm not like him—
obsessed with appearances
hoping others will
accept me
support me
vote for me
elect me.

Suddenly,
I want to rip off my dress
run back to X and press his body
hot against mine
feel his weight
      over me
      inside me
      carrying me
      off to another
          place
          time
          planet.

The crowd erupts in applause.
Miguel grins, proud supporter.
Balloons fall from the ceiling as
we stand up,
banners fly.

> *Who am I?*
> *How come my family had to turn out like this?*
> *Why didn't my mother live?*
> *Why'd she get ovarian cancer?*
> *Chemo?*

I paint the image in my head.
It's time to get back to my canvas.

The Scene

Headphones on
hands covered in paint
head wrapped around canvas,
I paint.

Melanie pets Missy
    purr   *purr*   *purr*
as I streak and stroke,
mash plastic-cup red and coffee-brown
forming a
    fast-paced   action-packed   messy image
of a guy standing in the middle
of a crowd of color.

It streams from the top of the canvas
raining down on his shoulders.
Sharper, more saturated hues than I've ever used.

Melanie says it looks scary,
yanks on my shirtsleeve
making sure I hear her.
I should continue to ignore her,
keep painting this party scene,
but I listen.

We're not at war—the two of us.

Me: He's nice. Someone sweet.
Melanie: No, he's scary.

I look at the harsh hues
strong strokes
but he's as cute as can be
isn't he?

Melanie: He scares me. I don't want to see.
She covers her eyes.
Melanie: Is he gone?

She uncovers her eyes, believing
everything bad can vanish
in the blink of an eye.

Weights

Melanie wants to paint stones
our stones
more stones.

She has memories,
her imaginary friend, Valerie—
        brushing Valerie's hair
        babysitting Angie Hippo
        swinging together in the park.
She wants to paint them in stone,
sock them away
in her underwear drawer.

Jane's unaware
her daughter,
    perfect   round   young
hides painted rocks
next to her panties.

But we can't go out now
dinnertime nears.
Instead, we sneak
into Dad's own private room
filled to the roof
      papers   posters   books
      folders   a globe   paperweights

his collection of paperweights,
presents from political people
seem an odd way to say thank you.
> *Good job, now here's a heavy object.*

We pickpocket the
> flat ones
> white ones
> round ones
> smooth ones
> big ones
> tiny ones
> lopsided ones.

More stones
now, our stones.

We Paint Paperweights

One for Missy,
          blue like a sky of potential.
One for X,
          red like lust.
One for Mom,
          pink like a ballet slipper.

Melanie accidentally paints over Mom's weight.
It turns gray.
The color of no color.
Me: It's ruined.
Melanie: I like gray. Like a day when the sun naps.
She kisses my cheek, then goes to work
on a bulky, round paperweight
content
determined
a part of Jane and also a part of me.

When Jane yells that dinner's ready
Melanie morphs into RoboCop
and races downstairs to munch on
          baked chicken
          boiled potatoes
          bland
          boring
          bourgeois

but then X calls.

Cracks, pt. 1

I throw on a thin skirt, socks,
and my Chucks.
Sandals seem so girly.

Dad: Don't stay out late.
Jane: We're handing out flyers tomorrow.
Me:

I'm sticky-hot,
full of baked chicken
and ready to escape this house, this heat.

To ease Dad's tensions
he hasn't met this young gentleman
X agrees to knock on the door
official date!

But X calls two seconds before I hear
BEEP BEEP

Try as I might,
    X won't budge.
Dad sips bourbon in his study,
                engrossed in political stuff.

Does he notice the missing paperweights?
Does he remember he planned on playing
the role of concerned father?

I slip out the front door,
hop in the recently repaired '88 Rocket.

X:	Afraid if I shut her off, she might not start back up.
Me:	
X:	Been in the poorhouse lately.
Me:	
X:	Can't afford another tow.
Me:	You're going to have to meet him eventually.
X:	Give me some time. I'm not too good with fathers.

He gives me that *cute boy* look.
I concede, but only because I'm not too good
with mothers.

Cracks, pt. 11

We roll down the street
bouncing along
split-open car seats
slightly ripped vinyl
coils and springs
years and years of people
in the passenger's seat.
> *How many girls have sat here with him?*
> *Jessica?*

Each bump
every pothole
lively swerve
sharp turn
seems my seat might
eject me.

> *Another bump, another girl?*

Suddenly, so insecure
I never used to be
like this with Ted
or with myself.

Is this what love is?
> A jerky   jagged   jumpy ride?

Cracks, Pt. III

Out in front of an abandoned warehouse
sheets like makeshift curtains,
wave out cracked windows.

X needs to make one stop.

The intercom button says   *Big Brother.*
We wait for an answer from   *Big Brother.*

The sidewalk's
chipped and uneven,
weeds fight through
the broken spaces.
Big Brother   buzzes us in.

I follow X up
three flights of stairs
stepping over old
bicycles
beer bottles
beams of wood
broken DVD players
doorknobs
and banged-up cardboard boxes marked
THIS SIDE UP.

At the top is that same guy:
      café guy   park guy   strung-out guy
looking a little less frazzled,
but still creepy, crazy.

Surprised, I step back
tripping over trash,
rotting stench.
The summer heat begins to burrow
under my skin.

X: Come on in. Don't be a baby.
Big Brother laughs.
It stings.
His words slice like paper cuts.
A baby?
I'm just a baby.
A naïve, innocent high school girl to him?

Me: I'll wait outside.
Whatever's going on in there
      baby or no baby
I don't want to see
like I don't want to know
about the girls with him
before me.
I'm not ready to know,
not steady, so I go
      clomp clomp
down the stairs.

X enters *Big Brother's* apartment
   creep creep
closes the door.

...
149

Cracks, Pt. IV

Clip
clop
clomp
        no one's coming after me.
Step
race
hop
        I rush to get out of there.

Am I a baby?

His words burn hot
truth sears.
Baby?

I push open the downstairs door,
fresh air hits me
like a muggy pillow
suffocating and cruel.
I plop down on a fractured piece of sidewalk
broken and split
as a tear falls.
Why am I crying?

I'm not standing up for myself.
I'm not taking a stand.
I'm just looking the other way,
walking away, crying.
Baby?

If this were a girl in one of my paintings, I'd title it
        The Pouter.
When X returns, I've painted a new portrait
        The Unaffected Female.

He snaps his fingers,
        claps his hands,
energy shooting out his palms.
Says he didn't mean to say *a* baby
meant *my* baby,
whispers in my ear,
his wet lips send chills down my spine.
I melt right there in his arms.

A new title for the painting of me
        The Girlfriend.

X: Ready to hear some music?
He loops his arm in mine,
I nod.

He kisses my lips
        gently
        sweetly
        tenderly
as if I were a baby
being laid down on a blanket.

His lips
        pillowy
        dewy
        soft
smell like Ajax
and air freshener.

What I See at the Show

Gavin meets me there.
We hang while X disappears
    returns   seems distracted   charged up
says this show
will pull him out of the poorhouse.
        The poorhouse.
A place he mentions a lot lately.

To get over George
Gavin and I play the *how 'bout* game—
Me: *How 'bout*... him? He looks cute.
Gavin: Bad fashion.
Me: *How 'bout*... the one by the door?
Gavin: He doesn't look a day over fourteen.
Me: It's an all-ages show?
Gavin: No side-bars. Next!
Me: *How 'bout*... the guy with the fedora?
Gavin: Not gay.
Me: Straight guys dress like that?
Gavin: No interruptions!
Me: Sorry.
Gavin: *How 'bout*... we get some drinks?

We secretly sip
        Jack & Coke & Jack & Coke & Jack & Coke
while the first band plays.

The music pulses through me
>swiftly
>swaying
>bleeding into me
>bold acrylic colors
>on a clean canvas.

I'm light-headed
>*must learn to control my drinking*
>*must learn to pace myself*

and missing X.

I run into Party Betty,
>a sparkling beauty in Jane's diamond studs.

I ask if she's seen X,
>she points to a door.

Betty: If you're into that.

What does that mean?

I jiggle, jangle open the door
>caught up in a rug
>only opens a crack

but it's enough
to see X on a couch beside
five other people
white powder
all over the table

spinning room
spiraling noise
expanding darkness
smell of cleaning fluid
mixed with *don't be a baby* and

X

his horrified face
signaling that I'm
seeing his secrets
suddenly I'm sick.

I try to act cool—*It's no big deal.*
I've seen it all before—*I'm no baby.*

I want to crawl into myself
ball up and hide
but the cleaning smell gets to me

and I vomit

on the rug buckled into a ball
by the door.

What I Learn at the Show

        I close the door and
idiot
        push my way through the crowd
stupid
        gathering in greater numbers
stupid me
        as the ticking minutes promise them
what
        their big-name band
on Earth
        their big night out
am I doing?
        their big, happyhappyhappy time together.

        And me,
silly
        vomiting in public
baby baby
   pushing my way out of the room,
   grabbing Gavin
        gasping for air
            grinding my teeth
      out on the sidewalk
  head between hands
elbows on knees.

As Gavin rubs my back, I tell him.
I feel sick, wishing it was just
a cold
a virus
I could catch and get over
a guy
I could dump and get over
but I care too much
hurt too much.

Gavin: So your boyfriend's a druggie.
Me: That's a little harsh.
Gavin: You're in love with a guy who does hardcore drugs.
Me: Cut it out. Maybe he can explain.

But I know, inside,
if he's hiding these kinds of things,
it can't be good.

Gavin: *How 'bout* ... we get you out of here?

What I Leave at the Show

SorrySorrySorrySorrySorrySorrySorrySorrySorry
SorrySorrySorrySorrySorrySorrySorrySorry
SorrySorrySorrySorrySorrySorrySorrySorrySorry
SorrySorrySorrySorrySorrySorrySorrySorry
flows out of X's mouth.

Swears he doesn't use

meth.

That was meth?

Says he was just hanging out, nothing less, nothing more.
X: It's not something big. If that's what you thought.
Something big?

Seems pretty big.
But he swears he

was

not

using

meth.

Should I believe him?
I want to believe him.
I want to love him.
I still love him.

Me:
Gavin: Meth?! Such a white-trash drug.

Like there is a hierarchy   of users.
A class system   of users.
An income bracket   of users.
Looking down on   other users.

Gavin takes me home.
He's—
              my knight in shining armor
              my valiant prince
              my protector.

Everything I thought
X
was.

I Am Not a Baby, I Am Not a Baby

here I am
here

there you are
there

between us
truth

around us
albatross

cheating me
cheating

you, smoking
gun
blazing hot
lit
by the summer heat
sniffed murky haze of
night snuffed out while

listening to music
rumors foolish.

but who? me
or you?
it's something big,
white hot
bang
knocking me over with
powder-strong force
liars and thieves
trample
my heart

shoot up
gunned down
in the midst of love
in the middle of lust
in the market of leftover
naiveté
gone.

blame the bandits of youth
robbed.

baby
baby
baby
baby
baby
baby
baby

me.

The Bad News

Coming home drunk
gets me grounded
for two weeks.
Summer without
      cell phone   parties   friends.

I…
should be ashamed
should know better
shouldn't embarrass the family
should never have been allowed out
      with that boy.

X gets
crossed out
of the picture.

Jane: Boys who won't come around the house are boys
          that are no good.
Dad: Last thing we need right now is a family scandal.
Jane: Especially since the election's only a few months
          away.

One true word—
      Election.

Disguised as wise words to shape and revise me.
Words that mean nothing to me.
Empty, meaningless, words that
without X,
fall to the floor and lie there like a rug
crumpled up.
See,
I've been caught
coming home drunk.

The Good News

Coming home drunk
gives me time to paint
for two weeks.
Summer with
      new pieces   fresh hues   ready for RISD.

Does Dad remember he promised to take me to see the campus?
Does Dad remember he promised to talk to a college counselor?
Does Dad remember he promised to help carry my canvas?

One little word—
               Election.

He's caught up in big debates.
Forcing me to participate
from now
until the November election.

I have no say,
see,
I've been caught
coming home drunk.

The Reform of Ralph

April caught Ralph using something.

Everyone's doing it, right?
No big deal?

Her now-red hair
bounces as she shares how she caught
Ralph red-handed.
He had a change of heart.
He decided he liked her and wanted to date her so
he turned things around,
cut *that stuff* out.

Summer storms
breezy and warm
now April and Ralph are an item.
A drug-free item.

Things I used to share—
little letters of love
kisses coated with sugar
sweet nothings
side by side
walking down
summer sidewalks.

April shares with Ralph—
      slushy drinks
      sloppy kisses
      summer love
      heating up
      just as mine
      cools down.
I shiver.

Now,
oh, how
the tables have turned.

Texts

DAY ONE
X: *4give me*

DAY TWO
X: *need u 2 believe me*

DAY FIVE
X: *sam? plz…*

DAY SIX
Me: *y?*
X: *she lives!*
X: *y? cuz I'm innocent*
X: *cuz I miss u*

DAY SEVEN
X: *cuz I luv u*
X: *cuz it's no fun w/o u*

DAY NINE
X: *cuz u r crazy bout me ;)*
X: *& …*

DAY TEN
Me: *& what?*
X: *& it's what henri paul wud do*
Me: *paint me an apology portrait?*

X:	*if that's what it takes*
Me:	*I'm grounded*
X:	*I'll wait*
Me:	*2 wks*

DAY ELEVEN

X:	*look out ur window…*

Summer to Falling

Out there—
      hot   hazy   heat
steaming up from the pavement,
the sidewalk.

Out there—
      pretty   pink   hearts
forming a chalk path
to my sidewalk.

      Cars honk   radios blare   laughter flies
around bouquet after bouquet of flowers
red
up against a tree.
      resting   insisting   waiting

X
marks a spot, a path
leading to my heart
red
like the roses.

My heart leaps upon discovery.
Romance still lives
       in the air
       in my lungs
       in my heart
       in every petal of every rose
beside the tree.

I pick them up
carry them back to my room
smell their scent for the next
few days.
My rose-apology portrait.

After I serve my sentence,
the first thing I do
is see
X.

Thousands of Years ...

... could pass by like fearless nations
                                at war
                                at peace
                                in love
we are back
to life as we knew it
                beautiful
                floating
our own oasis of
Vespas flying down city streets
black coffee
walks along Division Street
vandalizing *VOTE HENDERSON!* signs
learning to play bocce ball
at the park where we swing
swoon
seal
our love for each other.

Cheesy
silly
summer fun.

Dating Up

Up since noon
love in tune

high in thrill
strong in will

bold 'n' young
come undone

deep in play
light in day

without care
each aware

Political debates?
Adventure waits!

Taller tree
vaster sea
more worldly
mon ami
stronger coffee
makes me
          a
          better me.

Meeting His Mom

We arrive in the western suburbs
        identical houses line the streets circa 1940.

Two-story homes with tiny patches of lawn
        white awnings, blue mailboxes
            flag up, flag down.

A narrow living room holds
        mismatched furniture, dead flowers.

A woman's voice calls from the kitchen,
        the scent of homemade hot sauce greets me.

She sits at the kitchen table
        hunched over bills, adding and sighing.

X kisses her cheek.
        She tells him she's making tamales.

We sit. We talk.
        My name. My family.

Her: Henderson? Any relation to the one running for
           state senator?

I cannot escape my roots
        even out here in the middle of the 1940s.

X visits the basement,
>   while I help mush masa.

Her: You have the most interesting eyes.
Her eyes burn into me like Lady Elba's hand on my chest.
Her: Oh, you must get that all the time, you're so pretty.
Not really.
Her: They're so big. I've seen your dad on TV …
Oh no, not this about Dad again.
Her: He's got tiny eyes. You must have your mother's eyes.
Do I have my mother's eyes?
See what my mother sees?
Her: I'm sorry, X always tells me I'm nosy.

She pats my hand in a comforting
motherly way. Her skin,
>   pale   soft   cool   delicate
like Mom's skin,
before the tests   before treatments   before "that time."

X returns, wraps an apron around his waist
his arms around his mother's midsection.
X: My two favorite gals.

She smiles, proud, loving, ready to
>   mix the spices
>   mold the corn husks
>   make the most of her time with us.

Suddenly,
the smell of cumin
and the coziness of this kitchen
make me see a new side.

X as

compassionate son
talented tamale maker.

X as

a partner in caring
as well as
a partner in crime.

If Tamales Could Talk

After we taste the tamales,
X
revisits the basement
hoists a very large duffel bag
over his shoulder.

X: Okay mama, see you in a week.

We leave.

Me,
thinking of what it would be like to
visit again.

X,
scrolling through his phone for messages
or something.

The secret nature of things feels funny,
and too familiar.

When we get back to town, he says
there's a party …
could be fun …
we should go …

When we get back to town, I remember
there's a political event …
won't be fun …
I have to go …

And my father's clause—
            Sam must support family in all events leading up
                to election
fresh in my mind
from serving my time
being grounded.

X tells me to blow it off, be with him.
My heart wants to, but my head wins tonight.
Me: I can't.
He stares at the steering wheel. Says I'll miss a great party.
So he plans on going?
Even after the meth, the sorrysorrysorry, pink hearts, red roses?

He drops me off in front of my house
as I wonder if he will ever meet my dad,
shake his hand.
Would it be better?
Or worse?

"So you're going?"
"I have to."
Whose words to whom?

We kiss goodbye
slow and sweet.
It burns a little
just like homemade tamales.

Vive Le Senator!

Tonight's soirée takes place
in a French restaurant.
> *C'est la vie, I'm not hungry.*

Miguel rushes around
thanking donors for their money.
> *Merci. Merci. Oh please!*

Dad gushes about us being
one big, happy family.
> *Quelle surprise, that's what he sees?*

I play along with *joie de vivre*
the more supportive I am,
the less he notices of me.
I hone my acting skills.

We sit at the front table.
Dad shakes hands with everyone.
> *Vive le Senator!*

Whose hand does X shake tonight?
Why would he go without me?
Why would he *want* to go without me?

I slurp my soup with Melanie
until Jane yells at us.
Queen Vanilla has a migraine.
Quelle horreur!

More and more people show up.
So many so, I become claustrophobic,
duck out the side door and
get some fresh air.
Vive la blah blah blah.

French Lessons

Outside, I call X.
It rings and rings and rings.
I leave a message,
something stupid,
sounding insecure.
Merde.

As I contemplate my needy state
I notice a guy smoking a few yards away
seeming equally as bored.

He looks interesting   avant-garde   Eiffel Tower tall.

I approach him for a cigarette.
It's the only thing I can think of—a cig.
I'm bad at smoking
worse at flirting
but, if X can party without me
I can try and smoke with a cute boy.
I brush a curl out of my eye
brush up on my French, say hello.
He turns around. I gasp,
Sacrebleu!

Ted.

He looks at me like I'm from Planet Lame.

He's   calm

           cool

           careful.

Ted: Think your dad will win?

Like this is what's primarily

on both our minds.

I shrug, say I don't care.

I look closer at the Ted *du jour*

          longer, floppy hair

          Chuck Taylors

          Long Live Anarchy bracelet

He's *au contraire* to the Ted I knew

          buzz cuts

          preppy shirts

          basketball obsessed.

The space between us feels tense, yet

for the first time ever—electric.

Did he become interesting, accidentally, over the summer?

A je ne sais quoi oozes out of him

like laissez-faire took over

his Type-A personality.

He asks about "the college dude" as if spitting out escargot.

I shrug.

> *How should I know?*
> *He's at some party not answering his phone.*

I start to ask about his girlfriend,
realize I have no clue who she is
I've been so wrapped up in
me and X.

He tells me her name, and that it's over.
I try to act casual, yet my stomach flops a little.
Was that a pity flop?
Or…

Ted: So is there a reason you came over to talk to me?
Me: Maybe. There a reason you're here?
Ted: Maybe.
Not getting anywhere, I resign.
Me: I should go back inside.

Ted mumbles something
about me looking all serious
like Madame Roulin.

I smile at him.
He knows Gauguin?

Smokescreen

Inside, I run smack into my father
and

Ted's dad: Your father tells me you're really focused
                     on those SATs.

I shrug.

Ted's dad: Good. The more you study, the more you
                     increase that X factor.

Yes, I'm focused on the X factor.

Dad wraps his arm around me
pleased, puffed up with pride
Henderson blood coursing through both of us.

Ted's dad: Wish some of your discipline would rub
                     off on Ted.

No wonder Ted's sporting
an anarchy bracelet instead of a basketball.

A woman shakes Dad's hand,
asks for a favor in return for her vote:
get the loud drug parties on her block to go—

        disturbing ruckus…
        reeks of chemicals…
        kids who should be in college…
        not carousing…

Dad agrees, whole-heartedly.
She gives her address
which sounds vaguely familiar.
Party Betty's house?
Sweating, I excuse myself.

Dad gives me a little hug,
asks why I smell like smoke.
I smile at his guests as if he's whispered something
sweet in my ear.

Alone, I check my phone
sixteen times
pit in my stomach
finally, one text from Gavin—
                    I hope LA crumbles into the Pacific!

nothing from X.

Positive Energy

Twenty-four hours later
            no word from X.
WTF?

Not one to sulk, I call April,
tell her about X and Ted.
Talk some sense into me!

What's going on?
Did something change,
            something happen
            at the party?

He just went to a party, and I didn't.
Is that a big deal?
Am I being a baby?
Do college girls get paranoid?
Or is this just high school insecurity?

Me: Tell me I'm not crazy.
April: You're not crazy.
Me: Did I misjudge Ted?
April: You didn't misjudge Ted.
Me: But Ted's changed.
April: It's possible.
Me: Then it's possible for guys to change.
Thinking of X.

April: Not all of them.
Reading my mind.

My friend's good at
            lifting moods
            igniting hope
            living in a Utopian
            reality.

But just to be sure,
she suggests we consult Lady Elba.

Lady Elba, Pt. II

Same red neon *open* sign.
Same triangle-sounding chimes.

Lady Elba: Ah, the Great Samantha.
Me: Ah, the Lady Elba.

She remembers me well.
I remember her words well.

Something big is on its way to your soul.
But, is *something big*, something good?

She peeks into the cards.
I seek her answers.

Cards flip, flip, flip
she tsk, tsk, tsks
then, fingernail to lips.

Is my *something big*, something bad?
Is my *something big*, someone better?

How did I end up back here
with
this illusionist?

Why did I come back
while
the cards flip, flip, flip?

once
twice

bad
nice

pausing on a woman that looks like a nun.
Great, I'm going to become a nun.

Me,
becoming a nun.
Me,
already undone.

Lady Elba: Ah, the High Priestess.
                 High Priestess means you have …
knowledge
secret knowledge

powerful knowledge
all-knowing knowledge.

Me: But, what about *something big*?
Lady Elba: That, I'm afraid, has yet to surface.

surety in her eyes
uncertainty in mine

the future is a mystery
a future of uncertainty

Lady Elba: The High Priestess, you ...
her hand on my heart
my head held up high
Lady Elba: ... are on a journey with
                    The Fool.
The Fool?

Lady Elba: Yes.
I'm starting to think that ...

Lady Elba: But you possess the answers ...
                    ... are stronger, braver, wiser than
                    you know.

Lady Elba: The Fool is your friend.
And so it is.

Part deux.
Strike two.

When will I be through searching?
I, the High Priestess, should know that much.

Surely this makes me
the Fool.

Thirty-One Head-Spinning Flavors

After, I enjoy a caramel cone as
Party Betty sneaks up.

Betty: You missed a great party.
She licks her mint chocolate chip
while wearing Jane's earrings.

They look better on her than on Queen Vanilla.
Betty: X was there...
            party at the Lab...
            never heard of the Lab?...
            a place anybody who's anybody...
            would know.

I've heard nothing from X.
My stomach
jumps   leaps   shoots up through my chest
my heart
thumps   beats   worries
            What will Party Betty say next?

Betty: I thought you guys were exclusive?

Her words funnel
    through my ears
        into my head
            around my skull
       down my spine
   between my eyes.
Me: Not really, why?

A casual lie
I did not know I was capable of.
A part of me jettisons out of my own body
replaced by the High Priestess.
April watches this tennis match.

Betty: So that explains why Jessica was all over him.
         15 Betty
Me: Yeah, X mentioned her once.
         15 all
Betty: Well, he was really messed up on pills...
         30 Betty
Pills? Stay strong, Sam.
Me: It's not like I'm only seeing X...
         30 all
I think of Ted.
Betty: And X doesn't care?
Me: Sometimes he gets jealous, but...
         40 Sam
Betty: Wow. I didn't know.

She lobs a large bite of cone into her mouth
game

     set

       match

goes to Samantha, the High Priestess.

I hide my aching heart.
Party Betty leaves.
April's in awe of my composure.

The High Priestess version of me won't play
      the fool
      the baby
      the high school girl left behind.

Although, I go
      back to my house
      up to my bedroom
      throw my face in my pillows
and scream.

Suspicions and Doubt

My moist
hot
breath.

My burning
wet
eyes.

The sham
        muffles my rage
        stifles my anger
        calms me enough to
reconsider Party Betty's statements.

Just because I haven't heard from X
doesn't mean
he's out doing awful things.

Just because Betty says it was X
doesn't mean
I have to accept it.

My guy?
The one who
        helps his mom make tamales
        laces my sidewalk with chalk hearts
        fills my ears with love songs?

Party Betty?
The one who
        wears stolen diamond studs
        parties with druggies
        rats out her own friends?

Why should I believe her?
                Why would she lie?
Maybe X can explain.
                Maybe Betty's mistaken.

Perhaps there's a
sensible answer
a missed call
forgotten message
deleted text.

Perhaps there's a
reason
alibi
excuse
…

                Oh,
                even my heart has trouble believing
the hope.

                The fact—
                It has been over twenty-four hours
                and no word from X.

Images

When I paint
everything seems clear   in focus.

When I blur an edge
suddenly the image   works.

If only life were that simple.

When I finish
my final piece for RISD,
Melanie and Angie Hippo   cheer me.

Melanie: Sometimes my eyes get cloudy,
           but the tears wash the sad thoughts away.

Most times, I don't even notice her.
How can she be sad, see sorrow?
People leave—
       X
       my mom
       how my dad used to be
but Melanie's always
       under foot
       in my room
       by my side.

Still no word from X.
It's like he's fallen off the planet.
> *Guilt, maybe?*
> *Anger?*

Gavin reminds me how *not-noble* X is being
says he'll always support me.
He is, after all
my go to
my Gavin.

Turns

Every brush turn
becomes my turn
U turn

Painting myself
180 degrees
away from the
me
stuffed like a cream puff
with jealousy
insecurity
obsessively
checking my phone
checking the clock
tick tock
turns out,
it's just not
me.

Tides are turning toward
me

turns out what I thought
was burning love
just might not
be so hot

embers of our spark
    blitzed   burnt   blown
out of the park
turning heads with their
flim flam
flop
into the dark.

Relying
on another to
cover me,
X's silence
smothers me

missing my mother
I discover
I'd rather be
turning away
turning a blind eye
turning my focus
to canvas
to college
to RISD
and back to me

a better me
a sister to Melanie
I can be
immediately.

Obviously,
the tables have turned.

A Sunny Sunday Morning

Like something out of a movie—
Jane makes pancakes
Dad reads the paper
Melanie sets the table

      orange juice   fresh cream butter
      blueberry pancakes   real maple syrup.

Have aliens replaced my family?
My stomach growls
I sit.
Maybe we're not so broken after all.

Melanie recites the alphabet
shovels up pancakes
drives them into her mouth.

Dad asks about my SAT studies.
I lie.
Unless the study guides start seeping in
while I sleep
I'm doomed to SAT failure.

I ask about the campaign.
Dad: Let's get through today. One blow at a time.
How cryptic.
Jane sighs, excuses herself, runs from the table.
Is she crying?

Melanie chokes on a giant bite.
I pound her back
and she spits out the half-chewed mass.

Hello?
Nobody notices
I've casually saved my sister's life over breakfast.
If only I could save myself that easily,
   unchoke
   undo
   rewind
   and replay
   where summer went wrong.

Dad has to drive Jane to the doctor.
Miguel has to finish up the roster for the next rally.

Me: Why can't she drive herself?
I ask with what I think
is a rather innocent tone.
Dad: Can't you just help out?
He pushes his chair
     storms off.

I didn't mean to …
Maybe we are broken after all.

Our perfect
delicious
sun-drenched
something Sunday special
breakfast.

How Things Were with Mom

When I was Melanie's age I used to
sit in Mom's lap
suck my middle fingers.

Dad used to yell,
> *You're too old for that.*
> *You'll wreck your teeth.*
> *Big girls don't act like babies.*

All of which I ignored
sitting in Mom's lap
fat as a cat.

My High Priestess, Mom
protected me from the
pressure to grow up,
act like a big girl,
worry over crooked teeth.

When I got older, I quit
sitting on Mom's lap
being a baby
letting her protect me.

But I never got over wanting to be
near her
touch her

need her.
Her scent of
Cover Girl pressed powder
Chanel lipstick
switched to IV's
hospital beds and vomit.

The yin and yang of my mom.
    My down-to-Earth   high-end tastes
    High Priestess ways   mom.

Oh, to be
near her
like her
with her.

Pondering Things at the Park

While Dad's driving Jane to the doctor
I'm staring at my phone
contemplating calls
running around with Melanie
at the park.

Remembering creepy friends
fearing druggie strangers
wondering how they knew my name
at the park.

Never questioning
never doubting
never sensing a pattern
at the park.

X leaving me at
       parties
       music shows
       his mother's
returning with
       excuses
       duffle bags
       strange people

Why do I let him lie?

If he
knows druggies
parties with druggies
leaves me for druggies
hangs out with druggies
visits druggies
        he's lying when he says he's
not a druggie.

        He's a druggie
        and I'm not going to be the fool.

Believe

Honestly,
        I can't believe
        in us.
        I was a fool
        painted blue
        instead of canvas colors
        true
        to the hues needed
        for the scene.
Honestly,
        it's too far
        where you are
        I believed in you
        not me,
        too bad
        now I see
        I do
        when I move on I
        move away from you.

Honestly,
       I feel okay
       whole of me
       I believe
       in it all.
       I've tried
       Ted
       dread
       X's bed
       there's nothing
       I can't be
       at RISD.
Honestly,
       I believe
       in me
       mine, I'm
       glorious
       vain glorious
       high school victorious
       away from notorious
       I'm college ready.
Honestly,
       I believe
       in me.

When I Visit His Apartment, pt. II

I walk in
shutting the door behind me.

The room reeks
of takeout and tennis shoes
half-drunk bottles of Pabst Blue Ribbon
bad manners and boorishness.
Piles of books make it look like
hoarders live here.

Paper plates decay into *Jawbreaker* albums
paint crumbles off the wall
the fern rots in the windowsill.
His roommates hang out,
wave *Hi* as I step over
the banjo case.
Where's the banjo?

X leads me to his room navigating through
the wreckage saying

Nothing

like a tune from a
washed-up country ballad, the silence
saddens my heart.

At last, I've figured out
this song
this boy
the lies
even when he looks at me
in that way.
That way.

After we enter his room, he
sits on the bed
I stand next to his dresser
covered in coins and something sticky
we used to be giddy, gulping up
laissez-faire.

Me: I don't want to do this anymore.
X: Why?
Me: I'm tired of the lies.

Our eyes pour into each other
I want to melt, but I can't
see past
the dirty clothes
baggies of meth
and unmade bed
in his room.

This is it, I think,
and I don't believe in anything anymore.

Tears of Change

X: It's not what you think.
Me: I know about Jessica.
X: I love you, and—
Me: And what? AND Jessica?
X: It's not like that.
Me: Then what's it like?

He fumbles, nervous, quiet.
Only guilty people are nervous. Liars. Cheaters.
I will not be the Fool.
Every second ticking by
I just want to die.

X: I don't love Jessica.
His long, beautiful fingers,
wrap around a towel.
The same hands that wrapped around
            my face
            first kiss
            my waist
            his embrace
            stroking my hair
            touching my shoulders.

X: I do it sometimes…
            drugs…
            but mostly I sell…
            to people like… Jessica.

X breaks down.
Sobs into the towel while I try to stop the room
from spinning.
Says he's sorry about the lies,
that he told them to save me,
protect me.
Confesses he
    sells meth
             dabbles in coke
                      pushes a pill or two
                            needs money
                                needs me
                    knows he's weak
            hates himself
    less so
when he's with me.

Didn't want me to know because he thinks I'm
              perfect   beautiful   smart   talented
nothing like him.

Hearing these things makes my
              energy   rage   anger   insecurities
slide down his bathroom drain.

X: You and me, Sam. That's all I ever wanted.
Me: I don't care about the drugs.
          my anger   my stand   quickly losing steam
Me: I care about the lies.

His weakness deflates me,
corrodes my brain as we
hold each other and I see,
            while the drugs scare me
            it's not nearly as much
            as the distance they create,
            the lies and deceit.
This is what I believe,
honestly.

But SELLING?

He swears he'll stop
if I promise not to leave.

As he wraps his arms around me
big
strong
close
I feel we
are yet again
meant to be
like serendipity like floating downstream like good ole Henri

like love works.

places

After the fight,
our relationship takes a turn.
I've found my place
my role
protector, mother hen—the new definition of me.

If Mom cannot be this to me
I can be this to X.
It's what Lady Elba meant for me,
the High Priestess.
Still, I await my *something big.*

X and I find our new stride,
it feels right
and strange.

Like a bird unable to fly
or balloons caught in a tree

time turns.

Jane gets headaches daily
Melanie will only talk to her invisible friend,
Valerie
Miguel nags me
Dad ignores me
Ted begins texting me
April is now a blonde
Gavin,

>my Gavin
>my guide

stops talking to me.

>Says I'm a fool if I think X can change.
>Doesn't have time for foolish people.

Tips his hat, leaves me
with his half of our banana split
in Thirty-One bittersweet Flavors.

But the Fool is my friend, right, Lady Elba?

How Smoke Burns

Lying around in X's bed,
nestled up in the crook of his arm
watching him smoke
                    in and out
thinking about how we're
                    in and out
just like that smoke.

       falling in love   *in*
       lying   *out*
       making up   *in*
       fighting   *out*

Cigarettes.
The only habit he's kept.
I'm about to turn into
Sam, High Priestess, mother hen,
lecture about what he actually rolls in them
when he looks at me
       a look I recall
       a look I remember
       a look before he called me
       a baby
I shift my weight   lift up my arm   grab his cigarette
take a
   long
       slow
           draw

choke from the sheer power
of his home-rolled cigarette.

X laughs,
reminds me that Dad would die if he caught me smoking
because I am not a rebel,
I'm reputable.

We Hendersons have a reputation to uphold…

His words   inhaled in, blown out   make so much sense.
Where's the Sam that wanted to
     try things   experience life   all of it?

All of It

With the good comes the bad.
But is the bad really so bad?

How bad is bad?

Like lonely break-up bad? Or smiling-at-every-rally bad?
Worse than being called a baby?
Played like a fool?

How bad is bad?
Inferior to a boring step-mom?
Living without my mom?
Loving a boy who loves drugs?

How bad is bad?
Can it eliminate friendships? Take father from daughter?
Cause cancer?
Is bad poorer than a political promise?
More repulsive than lying?

How bad is bad?
And if I like it,
does that make it good?

How bad
is

bad?

...

Consulting April, pt. II

PickupPickupPickupPickupPickupPickupPickupPickupPickup

April's phone goes into voicemail.
>*I'm out with my man. Leave it at the beep.*

Since when is Ralph a man?
A
>clueless boy—yes
>lazy guy—sure

but man?

I try again.
This time she picks up.
I plop on my bed, get comfy.

April: Wanna do something later?
Me: I can't.
I mumble something about X.
April: Because you're a couple again?
I mumble a *perhaps*.
Me: Thought you of all people would understand.
April: I want to, but he's—
Me: Trying to change.
April: Trying?
Me: Maybe it's not so bad.
April: What did I tell you about boys and drugs?
I quote our cafeteria conversation.

Me: People who do drugs are lame.

April: Good. So we agree.

Me: But not all drugs are bad.

Me: Some save lives, you know.

Me: Cure cancer even.

April: Right.

Her voice trails
    sounds so far away
              like a fuzzy, unfamiliar connection.

She sighs.

April: Look, are you okay?

I touch a dried-up rose petal beside my bed.

One from X.

From the sidewalk. It's delicate.

And beautiful.

Me: Yeah, I'm good.

Consulting Gavin, pt. II

Gavin: You leave him yet?

Me: You left me with your ice cream sundae.

Gavin: And you left…?

Me: It's complicated.

Gavin: It's simple.

Me: You should try being more forgiving.

I'm thinking of George.

Gavin: You should try being honest.

Me: What's that supposed to mean?

Gavin: He does drugs.

          Which means he is a druggie.

          He tells lies.

          Which means he is a liar.

Me: People can change.

Gavin: If you choose not to see it, at least admit
          that's your choice.

Me: He needs me.

Gavin: I love you, Sam, but—

Me: Why do you always see the cup as half empty?

Gavin: Because right now, that's what the cup is.

Me: Just because George left for the summer doesn't
          mean he left you.

Gavin: Honey, lonely is lonely.
          And you can lie to yourself all you want.

          My Gavin
          my gadfly.

Where It Begins

Party Betty strikes again.
Big Blowout at Betty's House!

I decide we should go, thinking about
The Cigarette Effect.

X perks up, looks at me differently
like I'm surprising
interesting.
I'm feeling good until we're at the party and he
       runs into friends
       walks away
       avoids looking at me.

Being good, being the
       High Priestess
       mother hen
       reputable one
doesn't seem to be working.

So when someone passes around
    a bong   then some pills   then who-knows-what

I start my reputation anew, livin'—
The less-than-stressful life.
The paint-my-own-fate life.
The floating-airy-on-top-of-the-world-feeling life.

The back-next-to-my-guy life.
I'm surrounded by friends
so much in love and finally...
...livin' my life.

How It Continues

The following morning's
loud
light
less than fun,
feels like a dog
licked the insides
of my brain.

I pad down the hall
in search of
        aspirin
        water
        ice packs
        anything to stop
          the pounding
          the pressure
          the pestering pang in my gut,
          People who do drugs are lame.
          If you choose not to see it, admit that's your choice.

Instead of comfort, I find
Jane jabbering
Melanie blubbering
something about breakfast.
Melanie: Brewberry pancakes.
Jane: Daddy had to eat with his campaign people.
Melanie: Brewberry pancakes!
Jane: How about pancakes with Daddy for dinner?

The pounding in my head
burning in my eyes
makes me continue down the hall,
pushing past Melanie's
          Brewberry pancakes for breakfast! chant.

The thought of food
makes me queasy.

The thought of Dad
    off promising pancakes
            on the campaign trail
makes me sicker.

My head finds relief moments after
I take some Tylenol.
My heart finds relief seconds after
his call.
X: I feel so close to you right now, Sam Henderson.

I smile deep in my heart as I listen to his voice—
          warm
          soothing
          calm.

I frown as I find a note on my dresser from Miguel—
          Your father asked that I remind you to
          iron your dress before the next rally.

I ball the note in my fist
and lob it into the trash
like flipping a hotcake over a skillet.
Me: Wanna grab breakfast?
I ask,
as Melanie's chants grow louder.

He agrees to meet me
in twenty minutes.
                    Leo's Lunchroom.
I throw on my Chucks
and jog down the stairs
hungry for his touch,
starved for his smile.

Closing the front door masks
the sounds of my little sister
and her
flapjack disappointment.

            Brewberry pancakes! Brewberry pancakes!
            Brewberry pancakes! Brewberry pancakes!

Where It Goes from Here

From here
my dear
I'm up
                  up!
on top of the world

day after day
night after night
to lean on.

It's good
crystal clear
          up here

painting the feelings of my soul
dancing like I've got no control.

What's the fun in feeling safe?
Where's the safe in feeling fun?
Is this what I've been denying myself?

I swallow
          and suck
                    sip
                      and snort

and then

I lean on

X,
my rock.

I'm powerful
                and beautiful and
bohemian
full of vigor and vim
right in line
leaning in time

with X.
                Super Samantha Significant

leaning on

the counter
                spinning, twirling
                        becoming alive
                                livin' my life.

Blink blink
I drink
        sniff
            think
                up!

Flying High

You ready? X texts.
Quietly, I slip out of the house
3 a.m.
learning myself
liking myself
leaving for another adventure,
I grab a sweater.

August in Chicago's the hottest
time of the year, but early mornings
can be chilly.

We fly up and down
the empty city streets
while others live a dull life
   sleeping   breathing   in and out
the dim nothingness
coursing through their veins.

We will careen   in and out   of adventure.
Another Vespa, another pill
feeling awake and in awe of the
        heightened colors of trees,
          dewy hues kissing the crosswalks
a real live painting, better than I could paint.
It's the wee hours and I'm
    awake   alive   alert   alongside my favorite

kindred companion.
X shifts gears and the motor   juts us forward
                                          one-stroke
                                          two-stroke
                                          engine roaring
                                          racing to our destination.

We have a destination?
A point of no return?

A permanent smile wraps around my face
I wrap my arms around X.
He speeds forward, swaying   side to side   stops,
shh!
takes off his helmet
throws the Vespa in neutral.

We Put It in Writing

We glide the bike up the alley
to the back door of a building.
A motion light flicks on.
Ah!
X opens three locks with a series of keys.
Head spinning, stomach
        flip
                flop
        flip
                flopping
I watch the flickering light
standing under
a loose light bulb
        flick
flicker
        flickery
shining down on me.
X kisses my cheek
        dim, bright
        pretty light
waves me to step inside.
        Bye-bye little light!

Inside, I recognize
the back entrance to Café Hex
        where he works
        where I watch him
        where it all began.

The room rests peacefully amid
pounds of coffee, a humming refrigerator, shiny washed
vinyl chairs, lacquered tabletops that smell like Clorox and
coffee beans.
Must be what the circus feels like when the
audience goes home
packs up leaving
the bearded lady
all alone.

I spin
round and round
round and round and round
round and round and round and round
enjoying how the red walls blend into the yellow ones.
He watches me twirl closer and closer to him,
eventually, he pulls me in.

Me: This is breaking and entering.
I tease.
X: Not when you've got a key.
Me: You're very clever.

We kiss, hug, dance
eat day-old muffins
from the display case,
drink cold coffee.

I find a chalkboard
and draw a girl holding onto a bird
as they fly toward the sun.

X finds a permanent black marker
and writes, *I love you, Henri*
on a chair
on the counter
on menus
on my arm.

Officially, his pet name for me.
Gauguin would be happy.

This begins a correspondence
with each other's skin
on a secondhand couch
in the back of the café,
we tell each other the story of our hearts
writing and kissing
peeling off layers of clothes
in search of more places to pen
our love.

Eventually, we run out of skin
and the whirling, twirling, freedom I felt
at the beginning of this journey
fades.

Exhilaration replaced
with a heavy desire to sleep.
Nestled in his arms,
warm in his embrace
lying on the haggard couch,
I give in and sleep.
   Sweet dreams.

It would be
a dull life
without him.

In the Harsh Light of Day

The next morning,
a hand grabs my arm,
yanks me off the couch.

Man: I'm calling the cops!

The owner.
He shoves my shirt at me,
points to X—
Man: You're fired!

We dress while hearing—

Man: I'm pressing charges.
           You're a disgrace.
           How could you have such lack of respect?
           Look what you've done to this place.
           Look what you've done to your skin!
and worst yet—
Man: Aren't you Henderson's daughter?
           I've seen you on TV.

Even with X, I can't escape
being a Henderson.

Caught

The owner
dials the police
or so he pretends.
X doesn't want to stick around
to find out.
Says they can't book us if we're not here.

Really?
I've never been in trouble before.
Not like this.
So I follow X's lead
sneak out the back
half dressed
partially unzipped
mostly tense
fully freaked out
while thinking

> *Was the damage that bad?*
> *Didn't seem so last night.*
> *Will I go to jail?*
> *Breaking and entering is illegal.*

Even with X, I can't escape
fearing the future
Senator Henderson.

Outside, the Vespa's Gone

X kicks the side of a building,
curses about
the poorhouse
his bad luck
unemployment.

My phone rings.
Miguel.
   Crap!
My Dad's rally.
I totally forgot.

I shove my phone in my pocket,
unanswered,
realizing that
in the harsh light of day
I could be grounded
yet again.

Me: I better get home.

As I start to run off,
X points to my skin
covered with words
tracked up and down
  my arms my hands my feet my legs my back.
I'm a mess.

He convinces me to
        take a breath
        take a minute
        take a shower.
His place.
His argument ends with a
peck on my lips.
        Who can say no to that?

Arms wrapped tight
around each other's waist
we walk to his place
like Siamese twins conjoined
at the heart.

Coming Clean

I scrub and scrub,
barely fading the black letters
strewn across my body,
our love letter.

I should be freaked out,
            Will the owner press charges?
            Will he name names?
            Could I go to jail?
Instead, I take a long breath,
under the spray of water
and read everything—
            Paris or bust!
            You + Me
            This is just the beginning
            You're my favorite drug
            Who says drugs are bad?
I smile at that last one, the drug one.
Why'd I get so uptight about everything?
How bad can drugs be?
We're closer now, him and me.

Besides, I did them last night
            and the night before
            and I'm still here
            and still alive
            and unharmed.

X is right, this is just the beginning.
I step out of the shower.

Me: I love you.
He kisses my cheek.

What Also Comes Clean

The weight of the morning
slips away with X's kiss.
That is
until my phone
rings again.
Miguel again.
This time I answer.
Me: I'm not going to Dad's rally.
              Just leave me alone!

Miguel: You better be thankful I haven't left you alone!
His voice isn't calm
as usual,
it's rushed,
sharp.
Miguel: You're one lucky kid, Samantha Henderson.
Words spray out his mouth
like shots fired.

I hear only one.
Me: I'm not a kid.
Miguel: You sure you wanna go that route?

He tells me I should be
more concerned with the lucky part.
Lucky that X's boss called the cops
instead of calling the papers.

Miguel: Officer O'Neil is a friend of your father's.
Tells me how he
got the whole thing
squared away so Dad
will never know my
"criminal activity."
Miguel: And thankfully, neither will the papers.
          This shouldn't hurt your dad's campaign.

Most of me is
     happy   scared   thankful   relieved.
Most of me.

The rest of me
doesn't care
about reputations
or keeping my record
squeaky clean.

Me: Know what else won't hurt Dad's campaign?
          Me. Not showing up to any more rallies.

Miguel: I can't tell him that.

Me: Make something up
          like all you politicians do.
          Heaven forbid I tarnish the reputation of
          the Senator for the People!

What I Do for the People

I could run home,
give in
fold.

I could turn around,
be polite,
retreat.

I could beg Miguel
not to tell,
surrender.

I could be Safe Sam,
Ho-hum Henderson
Sweet Senator Hopeful's Daughter.

But if I want to be
the me that's
carefree
I cannot
turn around
look back
care
for rallies   strangers   promises   lies.

I can only
care
for X
and me.

Dad chooses to be
for the people.

So I choose to be
for the people
of me.

Instead of Rallies

X: You ready?
Me: As I'll ever be.

Night after night
we stroll
for the next few days
party
drift and roll
up to Logan Square
down to Pilsen
Ukranian Village
back to Bucktown.
I'm the belle of the ball
for the people of the party.

Most nights
I'm too high to care
that I'm not where
Dad thinks I should be.

Most nights are
like tonight.
We come and go
start and stop.
I think nothing of it.
Happy to be anywhere
with X.

X: I need to check in on someone.
Me: Check away. I'll be here.

I'm outside
    musing   smiling   dreaming   waiting
then
    ducking
behind the Vespa's back wheel
as Miguel
rushes by
            tousled hair   unbuttoned shirt sleeves
            tie flung over his shoulder
            on his phone   lost in words.

Miguel: I'm sure she's coming to the rally.
         I promise you I'll find her.
         Sorry, sir.

I watch him go
wondering why
he cares about Dad
so deeply.

X returns
         wipes his lips
         jumps on a new Vespa
and we begin

X: You ready?
Me: As I'll ever be.

Leave a Message — Gavin

BEEP.

Gavin: I'm not leaving a message.
           Where are you?
           Already left five for George.
           Okay, maybe fifteen.
           Fine. I called him thirty-ish times.
           Sam, he's leaving me.
           For real.
           Like, real, real.
           Hello? Sam?
           Can you just call me back?
           I need you to stop me from breaking fifty.
           Would seventy-five voicemails be crazy?
           Can't guarantee I won't do it.
           I might!
           Sam.
           Please. Stop. Me.

Leave a Message — April

BEEP.

April: Since when do I get the beep?
        Okay, so call me.
        I'm totally done with Ralph.
        For real.
        Like, real, real.
        Kaput.
        The problem with Ralph is…
        Well, you know.
        Anyway, I did it.
        I finally did it!
        I did the right thing.
        Did I do the right thing?

Leave a Message — Jane

BEEP.

Jane: Hello?
Hello, Sam?
I think this thing beeped.
My hearing's off right now.
Don't forget how you agreed to watch Melanie.
I have another appointment.
She'll be at the park down the block.
She's with her friend.
They also brought Missy, so make sure
they don't forget her.
I know it's only a few blocks,
but I don't want them walking alone.
Okay, Sam?
Okay.

Leave a Message — Miguel

BEEP.

Miguel: Sam?
Will you answer your phone already?
We have a problem.
A complication.
Your café incident.
The owner might've talked.
I need your help.
Your cooperation.
So your dad doesn't—
So your dad isn't—
Can you just please
call me
or answer your phone?

Things That Don't Come Clean

That afternoon,
I mull around X's room
humming a tune
waiting for him to return
from the bathroom.
Not wanting to head home.

I move his wallet and phone,
a book, a pair of socks.
I sit,
stare at the walls
stress about going home.
I've blown everyone off
skipped out on everything.
I'm going to be grounded for sure.

We Hendersons have a reputation to uphold.

    Disgust   fear   words   thoughts
swim around my head
as X's phone beeps
beside me.

A text.

Jessica: I miss you too. Let's do it again.

Texts and Subtext

The air knocks out of me.
I can't see
blurry from anger.

He lied to me!
He's STILL lying to me!

I rush around the room
dress
toss my wet hair up
search for my shoes.

X comes out of the bathroom
undressed
wonders what I'm doing
searching for my shoes.

He thinks I've spoken to Dad.
I tell him it's not who
I've spoken to
throwing his cell phone at him, the
text from Jessica
kissed up against his hands.

His stone-cold stare is enough for me.
I storm out of there running.

I give him no chance to explain.
Excuses are lame.

I run loudly
cry carelessly
wail effortlessly
hair sopping
ridiculous looking
gasping for air,
I turn the corner
passing by the park
and
        s   t   o   p.

I was supposed to pick up Melanie.

Park Déjà Vu

I race through the park
>   *Melanie!*
past the swings
teeter-totter
slides
>   *Melanie!*
>   *Melanie!*
through the grass
where we scoured for rocks
>   smooth ones
>   tiny ones
>   flat ones
our pockets heavy
our hearts light.

Me: Please be here! Melanie!
I stop.
My heart now heavy
this park empty
save for a few
hanger-outers
and
Guy: Hey! You, girl.
>   Sam!
the same creepy guy
X knows.
He sits sideways
propped up against a bench

    grimy
    yellow
    eyes aglow
    strung-out
    hanging out.

When I recognize him,
I rush to his side.

Me: Have you seen my sister?
           The little one? The one you saw me with
           last time we were here?

He inhales, long and slow
like he's got something,
information.

Guy: I'm not feeling so hot, you see.
           Could use a little pick-me-up.

He smiles like a crazy man,
holds out his hand

as if   expectant
as if   I'm connected
as if   the swap will set us both free.

Is this how he sees me?
A player in the drug scene?
I back away, disgusted.

Guy: Aw, come on. Just one packet.
           I might know something!

His words cut through me
like I'm a pawn
he plans to use.
This pisses me off.
My shock turns to rage.

Me: You're too high to know anything.
        I hate you. I hate everyone like you!

I turn from his hysterical laughter
and run home.

I've been used one time too many
today.

Summer's Fool

Priestess high
gone awry
how dumb was I?
cried dry

frozen hole
clenched cold
feelings fall
below zero

angers rage
lies ablaze
boiling stage,
turn the page

wide-eyed fool
high school
broken rules
cryptic, cruel

arctic hate
cut edge-straight
he devastates
x soul mate

frigid stone
frozen moan
empty phone
vacant home

heart breaks
head aches
hands shake
but mind
          awakes

me,
          the Summer's Fool.

What Fades Away

I come home to an empty house.
The family gone
for the next round
of shaking hands and empty promises.

I'm like this empty house.
Left my friends
for the next round,
of X's lies and empty promises.

On the table,
there's a note from Jane.
> *How could you forget?*
> *She's your baby sister and you*
> *put her in danger!*

Each time I try
to believe that I can be whole
> whole family
> someone who loves me wholly
> dreams of a full future, lie-free
reality sinks in and the truth of
how things really are
comes out.

How things really are.

Gavin was right.

Family Time

I used to love
sitting in Dad's study with Mom,
laughing at the giant portrait
of us on his wall.
Her green eyes, wide smile.

I don't love
sitting in Dad's study while he
screams at me
for blowing off everything.
His bloodshot eyes, furrowed brow.

Yells about
a united family front   his reputation   making him look bad

Yells about
shirking duties   forgetting Melanie   being a bad sister

Dad: What kind of person does that?
Me: I forgot I promised to pick her up.
Dad yells about Jane's stress.
The pressure I put on Jane.

Jane
Jane
Jane

I'm sick of worrying about Jane
my reputation
the rallies
primaries
posing for photos
pretending to care.
All the focus on him
and none on me.

What about me?
What about me?
What about me?

Family News

Dad: What about you? Let's talk about you.

Dad pulls a newspaper out of his drawer
opened to a particular page
folds it story-side up
throws it on the desk
in front of me.

His name,   *Henderson.*
My name,   *Henderson's Daughter.*
His title,   *Senator?*
Mine,   *Juvenile Delinquent?*

I ponder the titles and
the question marks.
The article mentions a
breaking and entering
at a local café.
Sites vandalism
         graffiti
              damage done
and
hush money handed out
like candy to quiet
a crying baby.

Me: I thought—

What did I think?

I try again.

Me: Miguel said—

Dad: Miguel no longer works with us.

Me: Why?

Dad: Because this is the very sort of thing he's
         responsible for containing.

Me: But he's—

I think about
the other day
         Miguel rushing, promising
while I eavesdropped, hid.
         Miguel calling, begging
while I ignored his plea.

I think about
how Dad always considered Miguel
a part of the family.
Our family.

I start to say
I'm sorry   I'm going to turn things around   I'm his girl
then I notice the new portrait
framed and hanging over his chair.

Jane holding Melanie
        larger image, thicker frame
the usual one of me and him and Mom—gone.
Miguel, my surrogate brother—gone.

Our eyes meet.
For the first time this whole year through
    dinners   rallies   SATs
I see my father how he sees me.

Me: I won't pretend to be your perfect Henderson.
Dad: You have responsibilities to this family.
Me: I'm not your family.

I point to the portrait.
Dad slams his fist on the desk.

I leave, hoping to never ever again see
        that picture of Jane looking down on me.

Getting It Out, Getting Out

Running up to my room,
I bump into Jane and tell her I hate her.
Really hate her.

Melanie peeks her head out
says nothing, quietly
closes her bedroom door.
>   *Who cares if I've hurt her feelings?*
>   *Or Jane's.*

I pack a light bag,
head to April's house, but
a bit of serendipity takes over
and I run into Betty.
>   *Who better to cheer me up than Party Betty?*

I text April, tell her I'll be by later.
She texts back.
April: I'm not your back-up plan.
>   *What does that mean?*
Radio silence.

I stare at my phone wondering if she's kicking me out
before I even arrive.
Then Party Betty asks if I'm just going to stand there
or have some fun?

No need to reply.
I throw my duffle bag over my back
and head to a party
with Betty.

Party Betty

Happy
    free
        changing in the bathroom of someone's house
I put my jeans on
    the tight ones
grab a drink
wash it down with a leftover pill
X gave me days ago.
The last remnant of him,
consumed.

I melt, feel
    prettier   funnier   relaxed   in control.

I've become a pro at this—the party part.
I can even do it without him.
I'm good at this. Better than I am at Geometry or Chemistry.
Halfway through my second cup
of liquid fire
my eyes begin to
    burn
    blaze
    burrow into the girl walking through the room—
Jessica.

Blonde hair cascading down her back,
curls falling in just the right place
bouncing against her flowery dress.

She doesn't see me at first,
which gives me time to form a plan.
I form no plan.

Only shove my half-drunk drink
into her dry dress.
She falls into the futon, screams.
I dive on top of her
            yanking her hair
            clawing her arms
            poking her cheek

twisting
      jerking
            raging
                  writhing
                        barely coming up for air
                  I cannot hear the
            shouting
      wailing
screaming

?:   Sam! Saaaam!

I'm
being pulled off of her.
I regain focus, burrow my angry eyes
into a face.

X.

Party's Over

Music screeches to a halt,
people gawk,
too drunk, drugged up
to form any opinions.

Taking my time,
    one second
            two seconds
                    three seconds
I hold my head high,
ignoring X's plea, *Why are you doing this?*
    a question too obvious to answer
and make my way
    through the living room
            down the hall
                  past the kitchen
                       out the door.
Done.
This chapter of me.
This person I've become—
      fighting   drinking   falling apart

speed-walking down the street,
turning around for a taxi,
thinking about X,
still in there
probably comforting Jessica
or

smoking meth
stealing a car
crashing a Vespa
ruining another girl's life.

I head to April's then remember she's
        not my back-up plan.
Another person I've pissed off in my
pitiful pursuit of livin' the life.

Instead, I head home, calling it a night
                                week
                    month
                                summer
                    life

Senior year is almost here
summer's done
and I
have got to get myself
together.

...
270

A Dream of Sleep

it's cold tonight
will I be all right?
or freeze from fright
no friends in sight

it's dark in here
I sit and stare
Gauguin's art, aware
Melanie's teddy bear

it's time for bed
what's in my head?
I gave up Ted
chose lies instead

it's rather late
who did I date?
didn't appreciate
must clean that slate

it's over now
I'll manage, how?
if friends allow
my humbled bow

sleep heavenly
sleep fatherly
sleep

I want to
sleep lovingly
sleep peacefully
sleep
deep
sleep
weep
sleep
please
keep

me in my
sleep

Summer's End

A week goes by without talking to Dad.
I don't have to go to rallies
I don't have to listen to people chant
     For the people, not payoffs!
He doesn't push or lecture,
just ignores me, too busy
taking Jane places.
     Where are they always going?

It's a mysterious side of Dad.
His new form of parenting—
     Ignore your child and she'll change.

Ever since the latest gossip
with Dad's opponent came to light
     —my scandal trumped by his—
I should feel free to
enjoy the waning days of summer
    roam   explore   shop
  think   create   relax   chill   enjoy
but I don't.

I'm trapped in my head
held hostage by my anger.

I paint   red   orange
                           yellow
streaks across canvas
    messy disorganized
               real
    understandable
                        angry
    lonely
paintings of my thoughts.

I feel deserted, betrayed,
and since I've got nowhere to go
          no boyfriend   no rallies
I spend most of my time in my bedroom
pretending senior year
will remake me
          here at summer's end.

News

Melanie visits me while I paint.
I've become her full-time nanny
as Jane and Dad traipse around town.

Melanie holds Missy.
Says she's not a baby, but Missy is.
Ironically, I know how she feels,
tell her she's a big girl.
She relaxes.
Melanie: Daddy's taking Mommy to the doctor again.

I peer over my canvas
pause
          rewind
replay.

They hadn't said *where* they were going or *why*.
They hadn't said *when* they'd be back.

Me: What do you mean?
Melanie: Mommy's sick.
Me: No, she's not.
Melanie: Yes, she's sick.

Her words stick, thick like they're stuck,
puffy and infected on Melanie's tongue.
She stares down at Missy, missing
my inquisitive look.

> *You're confusing your mom with mine.*
> *Your life is perfect. Your mom is fine.*

I think this, but seeing her
    face   clenched hands   squeeze Missy
I ache for her.
Remembering how Mom
   consumed   confused   completely capsized
me with worry.

I stroke her hair, try to slow her little-girl tears.
More than a dirty face that needs to be cleaned,
or a meddling sister I want to avoid,
she's a little girl, little sister,
scared and lonely.

> *Is Jane really sick?*

Thinking back on the Sunday breakfast,
pancakes and crying,
Janie avoiding my question about driving herself,
her doctor's appointment,
her constant headaches,
Dad blowing up—
it's all starting to sink in.

> *Maybe the pearls aren't so perfect.*

We snuggle like sisters.
Melanie: Is Mommy going to die?

Die?
People like Jane don't die.
People like Mom shouldn't die.
Then, people like me and Melanie
have to live—stuck.

I ask Melanie why she thinks this.
Tells me Jane
        has headaches
        getting her head "looked at"
        a big machine
        throwing up a lot.

I listen
hold Melanie,
we fall asleep like this
        paint drying on canvas
        tears drying on face
Missy returning to curl up
        between our legs.

Stereotyping Jane

and the headaches
and the pain
and the plain way she looks
and the way she makes me insane—
rubbing her temples as if
I'm so vain
and how simply she
replaced Mom like a
repairman swaps out a windowpane
and her name
Mrs. Henderson, not just
Jane
and the bland way she
walks
talks
speaks
eats her chow mein

and now I think that
everything I thought
and yep, I thought about it
a lot
and now, I think that
everything I thought

might not be quite
the same.

Mistakes and Identities

I tuck Melanie into her bed
kiss her forehead.
She mistakes me for Jane,
calls me Mommy
knocking the breath out of me.

Amazed at what it feels like
from the other side
I pretend to be
        a mom,
        her mom.
I play along so she'll sleep,
but I'm far from
        picture perfect
        poised
        larger than life
        in a portrait on Dad's wall.

I'm far from Jane
        controlled   contained
I'm far from Jane
        prim   plain.

I'm so unlike her, but
         do I hate her?
I wish I could take it back,
         I hate you
knowing now how it feels
to be kissed by Melanie and
loved like a mom.
Maybe my heart isn't quite so hard.

I pad back to my room
and paint two girls
holding hands
hopping happily along
carrying two stones
         together.

The Next Morning

I wake up early
        practicing for senior year starting next week
and make brewberry pancakes.

Things feel hopeful
better
not sick or somber
like a summer filled
with drugs and parties
shaking hands
alienating friends
hoping to win an election,
losing X.

Melanie bounces into the kitchen.
Dad finds his way in with the paper.
Jane…

I smile at Dad for the first time
in what feels like all summer.

Me: More syrup?
I offer, meaning
        I'm sorry for … everything.
Dad: Sure.
Dad says, meaning
        I know. I am too.

Melanie cleans her plate
Dad finishes his paper
Jane ...

I can be the bigger person,
head upstairs with some juice
            my truce.
The wooden stairs creak
under my feet
my heart pounding,
should I knock
or apologize
or turn around
and toss the juice
leaving things how they are?

Cracking her bedroom door,
She's on the phone.
Jane: I'll be fine ...
            don't want to be a burden
            like his first wife.

I remember
Mom's face, sick, sad, and swollen
I remember
her headscarf crooked, stained with puke
I remember
Jane's perfect smile pasted on the campaign trail,
and I wonder
if I bring her this juice do I want this truce?
She's not my mom.

She can take over the house, but she can't
            take over my heart
            take Mom's place.

I take the juice
            and toss it
                    down
                    the
                    drain.

Girls in Malls, Boys in Malls

This is a day of sorries—
> Dad
> April
> Gavin
> Miguel
> myself
minus Jane.

I clear away the formal apologies
with my two best friends, then
I clear my head at the mall.
Finally getting out of the house.

I learn April's new style for senior year is
> no longer Goth or gray
> blonde or blood red
but bookish
stepping out of the dressing room in a pink Oxford,
collar up.
I would laugh, but I can't piss off my friends
so quickly after making amends.

After fifteen texts
> ten tardy minutes,
I learn Gavin's new style for senior year is
> study-chic
> sporting boat shoes

and argyle sweaters.
Guess I didn't get the fashion memo.

I learn April
dumped Ralph for good
Deserved to be treated better.

I learn Gavin
stopped leaving messages
even more messages
for George.
They're just friends now.

Both my friends
            strong
            standing tall
            say they can   find better   do better   be better.

Senior year.
One week away!
They're
            excited, jazzed, thrilled, electric!
I'm still
            crummy, blah, broken, amiss.

They go into advice mode
April and Gavin: Go see Lady Elba.
                   Girl, you got to snap out of it.
                   What about Ted?

Nothing says, *I'm over it* like a hot
new outfit.
This is our year, our time.
This is your last shot.

Shot at what?
Becoming the senator's daughter?
Finding love?
Not dying alone?

I try not to be a buzz kill,
pretend the old Sam's back in action,
buy a few cute shirts, a new pair of jeans,
some argyle socks, even though I don't feel it.

Then leaving the mall,
we pass by a coffee shop.
The beans remind me of better times.
A sticker in the window says one single word—

LOVE.

Love

One word
with a picture of a goddess.
Maybe it will work if I buy it?
I comply, pretend the goddess is really
the High Priestess.
Me.

Gavin and April look at each other when
I'm paying, eyes judging,
saying nothing.

It will be my power mark.
          My strength.   My freedom.
                  My *something big*.

LOVE.

I am the High Priestess, reminded that
it's not perfect

LOVE.

But it's all around, waiting for me to take it
back.

Sam I Am

I am greater than a shoe size.
I am more interesting than a label.
I am deeper than an opinion.
I am more than a politician's daughter.

I am smarter than a test score.
I am more valuable than diamond earrings.
I am larger than a fashion trend.
I am stronger than a drug.

I am a cut above
priority mail
my own masterpiece
executive platinum
finer than bone china
blue ribbon worthy
senior level
VIP
leading lady material
I am all that and a sister-daughter-friend bag of chips...
...and

I am ready to love.

First Day of Senior Year

I make breakfast for Melanie
while Dad tends to Jane,
          walking and rubbing
          pacing and squinting.

I wonder
          Does Melanie see her pain?

At school, my locker's next to Gavin,
so I get to witness
          The Drama of George.
It replaces
          The Problem with Ralph.

I wonder
          Will Gavin take him back?

I'm back in school,
          preparing for college
          preparing Melanie's breakfast
          preparing to move on
and X is…?
It's just one more thing that separates us.

I wonder
          Will I ever heal?

Even though I should focus on my
           future   friends   family

All I can focus on is
           What is he doing?
           Is he still with Jessica?
           Does he sing Chesterfield Kings *in her ear?*
           Are they eating brunch at Leo's?
           Is she scrunched up next to him in the booth?
           Does he remember eating there with me?
           Does he even remember me?

I'm left here
           in the hall
trying to shake memories,

                            haunted.

In Transit

Like my academic angel,
Ted floats by,
grabs my arm and escorts me to
Senior English in Room 107.

He pulls out a box of Milk Duds, informs me that
nothing cures depression better than chocolate.
   How'd he know I was down?
He pops a Milk Dud,
chatters on about things not sports-related.

   Things I might actually care to know:
what bands are playing this weekend
how he's learning guitar, even wrote a song
who knew chords were so difficult?
And,
did I hear about the Gauguin show
at the Art Institute next month?
   The Yellow Christ.
My favorite.

Together, we walk arm in arm as
friends
students
fellow music lovers
art lovers
chocolate lovers.

But,
somewhere in the hollow of my heart
maybe it still might be
something more.

At Lunch

Gavin: So you and Ted…
Me: …are nothing.
Gavin: I don't know, Sam, he seems…
Me: …innamorato.
April pulls out a pocket thesaurus.
                How far is she going to take this brainy thing?
Gavin: In a whatto?
April: Smitten. In lurve!
Gavin: I believe our little girl's got a new boy.
He sniffs like it's touching,
our love story.
Me: Spare me.

I know what they're trying to do,
help me move on,
but is falling for the guy
you dumped junior year
moving on or moving backwards?

Gavin: I always liked Ted.
April: Least he doesn't dabble in drugs…

Ralph walks by, smiles,
then passes to sit with his new group
next to the
           new   cute   perky girl
unaware of *The Problem with Ralph.*

Gavin: Well, whatever's going on with Ted…
Me: You mean nothing?
Gavin: Just go with it.
He gets up,
leaves.

And as usual, he
takes the last word.

Week after Week after School

April, Gavin, and me,
we start a new routine.
We've crossed out our summer habit
of hanging at that café—haunted.
Instead, we study in the food court through fall
at the mall by April's house.
New school year, new start.

While pondering a geometric equation,
my eye catches the salon sign.
I stand up, pronounce that it's my time for a new look.

April: For reals?
I nod.
Gavin: Oh holy night! This girl's gonna look hot!

On the escalator to the salon, we pass
Party Betty weighed down with bags.
She waves, says
she heard I dumped Hef,
gives me a thumbs-up as we pass.
One going up,
the other going down
until she reaches the top.

Betty: He did it to all of us.
          You were just the strongest!
She holds up her bags
like that's her best way to cope.

Before I can say anything
Gavin grabs my arm,
pulls me into the salon.

Two hours later, I walk out
happily highlighted
          and ponytail free.

A new look
          a new me
                    and I
quite like it.

Election Night

       Dad's ahead in the polls, but behind
getting ready for his big night.
       Jane leans against the stairs, in pain
holding her head all night.
       Melanie hops on my back, excited
about babysitter night.

Jane notices my new hair, says it's pretty.
I tuck a strand behind my ear, about to ignore
her compliment, but thank her instead.

Dad changes into a perfectly pressed shirt,
shined shoes, sleek suit.
All of his supporters await news
       Henderson for the people!

Melanie and I paint stones
eat dinner
watch TV
wait to see the election results.

I deliver Jane some juice,
actually take it to her door
instead of turning around and tossing it.
She's writhing around, making no sense now
mentions
       Christmas
       glass figurines

cottage cheese
apple picking

mistakes me for Melanie
            tries to sit up
            falls back down.
She's scaring me.

Her flushed face
        sweaty   sad   delirious.
My last memory of Mom
        sweaty   sad   delirious.

While Jane's been playing off her headaches,
trying to be
            the perfect wife
            the careful mother
            the diligent politician's aide,
she's actually been
            the ailing wife
            the undiagnosed mother
            the weakening politician's aide.

I can't undo what I've said to her.
I can't even relive the mistakes
            thinking of Jane as Queen Vanilla.
I can't reverse what I've said or done.

But I can take control
                        this time.

Emergency Night

My fingers jitter as I call 911,
tell Jane they're on their way,
try to sit her up.

I place a cool cloth to her forehead,
tell her it's going to be okay.
She holds my hand
says she's ruining everything
and that she can't see the ocean,
wants out of this hotel
in time for Christmas.

I wipe her sweaty hair from her eyes.
She lays her head on my shoulder.
This might be one of the only times
we've touched.
Usually,
she's holding Melanie,
keeping her distance while I keep mine.

It feels good,
our closeness
    calming   comforting   caring   kind
like mother and daughter.

Could this be something I could have again?

Melanie rushes into the room
   sees her mommy
Jane
   disjointed and jerky
   spewing gibberish
Jane
   Melanie's mother
not my mother.

She starts to cry   recoil   cause a scene.
I tell her   *make Mommy proud*
   we're going for a ride
and I try to be
   mother daughter sister High Priestess
for everybody.

Diagnosis and Recovery

Doctors meet Jane, rush her
through double metal doors
as Melanie and me
walk by her side
> wondering
> worrying
> watching.

Jane grabs my hand
says she's sorry, didn't mean to let me down.
> *What does this mean?*

I try to ask, but her hand slips out of mine
and out of sight where they'll
> poke probe x-ray test scan

radiate her brain
review her paperwork and
rule out everything.

Sitting in a love seat
waiting in the hall
Melanie and me, together we
wait for more tests
> more doctors
> Dad.

Hours pass without any information.
I try not to panic.

Dad arrives just in time
to hear the news
from the doctor.
After all these months,
they've finally figured it out:
Central Nervous System Vasculitis.

Dr. Frank: She's going to be okay.
He pats my back.
Dr. Frank: You got her here just in time.
Melanie: Sam saved the day!
Dad weeps.
Says he couldn't take this again
that once is more than enough.
Dad: For you and me.
I agree.
Just feeling his wet cheek, knowing
he still

     remembers   misses   cares about Mom
somehow makes it okay

     to focus   worry   care about Jane.

Miguel calls to give us the news.
Me: I rehired him.
Dad smiles

     agrees,

         he's practically a Henderson.
Me: And you're actually a senator.

Dad scoops us up in his arms—my sister and me.
We visit Jane, hooked to an IV,
together we, Melanie and me,
next to Dad, *the new state senator*,
and Jane, are all one
little

family.

Chocolate Muffins

Another wave of medical staff rush in
      patient shakes   machines beep   people yell

      twenty-something female
      overdose

Jessica's gurney rolls by me.
X holds her hand
      lying there
      pale, unaware.
Doctors ask him to step away
they whisk her off.

His cheeks flush
      pink
            crimson
                    burgundy.

He
turns, tilts his head,
pushes back his hair
the way I've seen him do a hundred times before.
This one move reminds me
      my own hair
      gone   changed   new.

He
throws his arms over his head,
sighs. I see—
a rip in his shirt forming.
Soon, it will
      spread   tear   grow
form a long, gaping hole.

Suddenly,
I'm not sad for Sam or jealous of Jessica.
I remember that day,
that first day he plopped down at my booth
when I asked for a chocolate muffin.
       I want to learn about life—all of it.
I'd said it.
Now, I *am* learning about life—good and bad.

He
notices me.
His eyes swim with sadness
hoping to reach the shores
of my sympathy.

I
look away,
smile at Melanie and ask
if she's hungry.

She
nods her head,
sucking her thumb
and asks if we can get some
chocolate muffins.

We
stand,
holding hands
walking toward the doors
morning washing ashore
hope inside finally restored
looking forward more
than ever before,

I agree.

Acknowledgments

While this is a work of fiction, some real-life characters helped me make this book possible. And so I'd like to thank all the wonderfully supportive people who contributed to bringing this novel to life.

In no particular order, I'd like to say *thank you thank you thank you* to VCFA and my advisors who helped shape this when it was just a germ of an idea at Vermont. Big thanks to the Keepers, the BrainTrust, and my first, second, third, and millionth readers—you all rock. To my family, who've put up with my stories since I was ten. To my dad, who is nothing like Sam's, and to my non-fictional Gavin inspiration.

Thanks all around to Brian Farrey-Latz for seeing something special in this story, and to all the folks at Flux for their tireless support. To my agent, Erin Harris, and her never-ending enthusiasm. And last but not least, to Rob, who reminded me many a time that it was okay to write when I felt guilty putting everything else aside. I owe you a year's round of laundry.

© *Mary Sylvester*

About the Author

Stefanie Lyons holds an MFA from Vermont College of Fine Arts. When she's not writing, she's organizing her locker, crushing on boys, practicing her clarinet, or getting ready for prom. In her head, that is. Because her teen years were great. Stefanie resides in Chicago. *Dating Down* is her first novel.

Visit Stefanie at stefanielyons.com and follow her on Twitter & Instagram: @sllplatform.